SOMEWHERE IN AMERICA:

Situations of XX and XY

Sydney Molare'

ISBN: 0-9745188-1-6

Library of Congress Control Number: 2004102029

Second Publishing March 2004 by:
Fishbowl International, Inc.
"Viewing Life from All Angles"
PO Box 362
Roxie, MS 39661
www.fishbowlinternational.com

Printed in the United States of America
This book is printed on acid free paper.

As always, this book is for Gar. Forever my love…

SOMEWHERE IN AMERICA:

Situations of XX and XY

www.somewhereinamerica.net

TABLES OF CONTENTS

The Oldest Lie Ever Told   1

Pretty In Pink   10

Laying On of the Hands   16

Massage-a Twa...   26

And the Drama Goes On...   34

The Proof is in the Pudding   40

Moooooo Cow   47

The Janitor   51

The Notification   58

High Education   66

Dig-Dug-Dugged   73

On the Dole   78

The Show   86

Dumb and Dumber   94

Parent's Rules   107

On the Down Low   115

I've Been Loving You *Too* Long   123

No Rest for the Weary   137

Mercy Killing   144

Somewhere In America   153

THE OLDEST LIE EVER TOLD

Seventeen. Big belly. In high school. No job.

I know he really loves me, though. Man, we really connected. He just needs time to get use to the idea. I told him I was pregnant and he wanted to act like a comedian. "It could be anybody's baby," he said. Yeah. Like he doesn't remember getting my cherry at the Motel 7 on Hwy. 42. Like he forgot all the *begging* he did and the promises he made. Like I am some *tackhead* on the street, spreading my *legs* for every *taker*…STOP IT! That is a LIE! He loves me. He told me so. I just need to *calm down*.

He asked me to have an abortion. I was stunned at first, but I know he was just joking. I realized that this baby thing really threw him for a loop. He didn't mean it. He loves me. He told me so.

I mean, afterall, he couldn't just up and forget all the dreams we had — college for me, marriage, big house with the white fence, fancy cars and going places together. He couldn't renege on everything, as if he wasn't party to any of the conversations.

I know he will come around once the baby is born. Hell, I'll be the mother of his child and that means more than *any* of them skeezers trying to run him down. He's just a little shook up right now.

My Mama is no help whatsoever. All the time saying "I told you so. I told you a man that old ain't got no business even *talking* to a girl your age. You should have kept your legs closed. I taught you better. Well, this child is your child, not mine to raise." Makes me sick, all her preachings and going on.

Mama just doesn't understand and age *ain't nothing but a number!* So what if he is ten years older than me? He is mature, not like these chap-acting boys around here. I mean he has a *real* job and can take care of me. He will have to move out of his Mama's house and get us an apartment, but that no big deal. I will be sssoooo *glad* when he shows up to take me away from here!

My use-to-be-friends just point and talk about me. No to my face....but I know it anyway. They act like I got a disease that is catching.

My favorite teacher told me she was surprised and disappointed in my life choices. What was I going to do with my future? I proudly told her that my boyfriend was having some problems, but as soon as he works them out, he will marry me and make us a family. She just stared at me like I had three heads.

They don't *understand.* My boyfriend just needs a little time to get use to the idea of the baby then he will be *all right.* True, I expected him to come around a little sooner than this, but I am willing to wait because I *know* he loves me and he will love *our* baby. He told me so.

I call his house and his mother says he isn't home. I catch a bus over to his house and his mother says he isn't home, even though his car is in the driveway. *Hussy doesn't think I'm good enough for him.* I went to his job. I saw him working and tried to catch his eye, but I guess he didn't see me. I know he would have been mad enough to fight, if he had seen security escort me out the gates. I emailed him and the message came back MAILBOX CLOSED. I guess he doesn't check it often and it must be full or something. I'll bet he is calling me and my mother just isn't letting me talk to him. *These Mamas just don't want us together!* But, I know it is just a matter of time. Love will prevail. It always does. And my boyfriend loves me. He told me so.

I saw him at the grocery store with a red headed girl. At first, I got mad. When she went down another aisle, I just marched right up to him and got in front of their cart. His eyes almost bugged out of his head. I asked him who his friend was. He said she was his cousin who had just moved into town. He was helping her get some groceries and get settled that's why he hadn't been over there to see me. How was I doing? And the baby? He is going to call me tomorrow.

Tomorrow came and went and no phone call. He must have gotten tied up helping his cousin get settled or something. I'll bet he called and my mother didn't tell me again. You know, I'm just about ready to confront her about her trifleness.

Dog! My belly's big as a beach ball and my back hurts *all* the time. Another month to go and I can present my boyfriend with his firstborn child. I know he will be *so proud*. He will come to the hospital and take us to our new home. My Mama will have to pick her trifling tongue up off the ground and beg my pardon for all the nasty things she said. His Mama will come in so happy to see her first grandchild. They'll see.

I wake up one morning and my stomach is cramping something awful! I stumble down the hall to the bathroom, but I felt the pee running down my legs before I made it. *Damn, these cramps are bad*! My Mama hears me and comes out of the bedroom. She says, "Girl, the baby is coming!" I told her it was just bad cramps. You don't have bad cramps when you have a baby, do you? The pain slams across my belly again and again. Mama throws on some clothes and gets me into the car.

The cramps make me *holler* from the pain. I start crying because I *know* I am dying and my *baby* is dying and my boyfriend *isn't* here. I tell her to call him when we get to the Emergency Room. She just rolls her eyes

4

and keeps on driving like she doesn't see me over here *dying* in front of her face!

Those people at the hospital are no better. My mother told them I was in labor. I told them I had bad cramps and was dying. Help me! They just wheeled me up to a room and slid me onto a bed. A doctor came in and told me he had to check me. Afterwards, he explained that I was dilating normally and the cramps were part of helping the baby along to delivery.

CCRRAAMMPPP! I howl like a dog hit by a car. I am ashamed of myself. Nobody on TV acts like I am acting. Nobody said the pain was going to be like this.

CCRRAAMMPPP! Mama did you call him? You called two hours ago? Did you talk to him or his Mama, 'cause you know his Mama don't really think I am good enough for him.

CCRRAAMMPPP! Wonder what is holding him up? I wish he would get here. I *know* he wants to be here for the birth of his firstborn.

CCCCCRRRRRAAAAAAAMMMMMMMPPPPPPP! I can't breathe. Mama I'm dying! Get help! Mama just continues to pat the sweat off my forehead and nods.

PUSH! They tell me.

PUSH!

Don't they know I can't have this baby until *my boyfriend* gets here?! He *wants* to be here! My Mama tells me to "shut the hell up and *PUSH!*"

PLOP!

Instant relief.

A baby is crying. *Our* baby. They take it away! My Mama says they'll bring it back in a minute.

I am *hopping* mad! We could have waited until my boyfriend got here. Now he is going to be disappointed he missed it all.

Here they come with my baby. Mama, this baby don't look like nobody we know! They made a mistake. They have mixed my baby up! "No mistake," Mama says. They slap a bottle in my hand so I can feed the baby.

Have you heard from him? Is he in the hallway waiting? "No," Mama says. Well, he probably hasn't gotten the message yet. You wait and see. He'll be here. He loves me. He told me so.

Three more days of feeding, changing diapers and walking a crying baby. Mama just went home and left me here. My boyfriend hasn't shown up *yet*! What is *keeping* that man?

Mama shows up on the fourth day and drives me home. I ask her to drive by his house so I can show him and his Mama the baby. She says "No. They know the address."

I march into the house and call over to his house. He answered. I tell him I had the baby and ask when he is coming over. He mumbled, "Wrong number," and hung up the phone! I called right back and the phone line was busy. I guess I must have misdialed. Boy, I really shook somebody up.

Day after day, I have to mix formula, change doodoo diapers and figure out why this baby is crying. I cry right along with the baby. I dial my boyfriend's number time and time again, until one day there is a recording saying the number has been changed to an unlisted number. When the baby is old enough, I'm going to go over to his house. They didn't tell him I'll bet. He loves me. He told me so.

Finally, I can take the baby out of the house. I dress him warmly and hop on the bus. When I reach his house, I see his car is in the driveway. Good. He's home. I ring the doorbell and the red headed cousin answers. I tell her I would like to see my boyfriend and tell him about our baby.

"Boyfriend?" she looks at me puzzled.

"Yes. Tell him I am here." Before she does, I hear him in the background coming to see who is at the door.

His mouth drops open when he sees me. A smile lights up my face. I hold the baby out to him. He *doesn't*...take...the baby. The red headed cousin asks

7

him who I am. He begins to stammer and stutter. I turn to her and proudly proclaim that I'm the mother of his child.

"What?!" she yells.

She tells him he better start talking and talking… right… now! I told him he didn't have to explain our business to his cousin.

"Cousin?! Cousin?! I am his *wife*!" She gets in my face and hollers.

I almost drop my baby from the shock. He pulls her back into the house and slams the door. The yelling reaches me, a portrait in shock, on the porch.

Wife?! How in the heck can he have a *wife*? *We* were supposed to get married! He told me he loved me! We made plans! I know, that is just some wannabe tackhead lying about being his wife!

Nagging doubts assail me.

Then, the undeniable truth slaps me in the face.

DAMN, GIRL, SHE AIN'T LYING! HE'S THE ONE BEEN LYING! He is *married*. She ain't no *cousin*. *YOU* THE DAMN FOOL!

I feel the hot tears course down my cheek and onto my baby's face. I shuffle down the steps and run down the street to the bus stop.

I cry the entire way home. My baby cries with me.

How could I have been so stupid? What am I supposed to do now? I didn't finish high school 'cause the baby came. I don't have any money and my Mama says she ain't gonna be no full-time baby-sitter. What am I going to do…?

Well, ten years have gone by and my old "boyfriend" never darkened my door. Not even once. Never sent our lovechild a penny. No cards or presents. He got transferred shortly after the day at his Mama's house. I found out later, he had been married for five years before he got me pregnant. I tried to get child support, except we could never find out where he was.

Me, well, I got my GED, but the closest I ever got to college was the job I got cleaning the dormitories. I'm not married either. Oh, I got close (I think, anyway) but nobody was willing to raise another man's child. And yes, I'm still living with Mama. I don't make enough money to live anywhere else. Kids cost money, you know.

He loves me. He told me so.

NOT!

PRETTY IN PINK

"You sure are an ugly girl."

Huh? Was that kid talking to me? I swiveled my head around and saw a little boy of about six staring up at me.

"What did you say?" I asked indignantly.

The kid just looked at me then ran off to his mother at the end of the grocery aisle. He pulled her towards him, whispered in her ear and pointed at me. She looked up the aisle at me, grabbed the kid by the jacket, did a wheelie with her cart and pushed away from me.

Jealous.

Just plain old jealousy.

People are always jealous of me and they should be. I *know* I am looking as fly as can be. Shoot, I'm 5'11'', trim and slim. A *fine* physical specimen, if I have to say so myself. I've got on a gorgeous pink jersey outfit that fits me to a "T" with matching Gucci shoes and bag. I just got my hair done up at Butcheros in my favorite "waterfall" and my makeup is flawless. Now, once I have the surgery to get rid of this big old Adam's apple, I just don't think I could get any better. Just jealousy. Plain and simple. Shoot.

I pull my cart up behind an older lady and wait patiently while the cash-register-challenged cashier rings up the purchases. I spot the lady with the kid in the other lane. The kid is staring again. I turn my back to them. They make me sick anyway. Always somebody trying to ruin my day.

Forget them, I tell myself. *You know folks been misunderstanding you since you was thirteen.*

Now thirteen is when I broke open the closet door and announced to my family that I was really a girl. No, didn't nobody mess with me or nothing. I was a *girl* and I was sick and tired of them acting like I was a *boy*. To say all hell broke loose, is to downplay the reality of the events. My Daddy punched me like we was in a title bout. Then my Mama got into the act, crying and screaming and slapping my face. Man, I couldn't been seen nowhere *near* a school for two weeks.

When I left home, I let the "real" me shine brightly. No more Levi's and boxer shorts for me. I wanted something soft next to my skin like that lingerie I saw in the Victoria's Secret store at the mall. And since I couldn't get any help selecting and trying on clothes in the women's section, I found me a good seamstress to make all my clothes. This dude does a great job too. Fits my stuff snug, just like I like it. In fact, he made this sharp suit I've got on.

At first, the name-calling made me want to fight all the time.

11

Faggot.

Punk whore.

Beotch.

If I *thought* you said it, I was trying to be all over you like white on rice. Needless to say, some of them suckers beat the crap out of me. A few of them tackhead women did too. But, I realized I had to protect my face. I couldn't be walking around all the time scratched up with black eyes and so on. My face is the first thing a potential "partner" sees. And I want him to be *happy* with what he sees.

Forget it, I tell myself again.

Dang! Now this little old lady can't find her money. Why did I pick this line to get in? Sheeeit! Miss Cashier Challenged 2002 is just standing there drumming her three 1/2-inch nails on the countertop. Damn! The old lady is putting her purse junk on the countertop. This could take all night, big as her damn purse is! I look around at the other lanes, but they are just as crowded.

"How much do you need, Ma'am?" I asked politely.

The little old lady looked at me then went right back on scrounging in that purse of hers. *NO SHE DIDN'T!* I look at the cashier and she has a stupid smirk on her face. I wanted to kick that old lady in her ass right then and there. I take a few deeeeepppp breaths and wait. Patiently.

"Here it is!" the old lady holds up the money triumphantly. Good damn thing too. I was just about to leave my cart and the food piled up on the conveyor belt and walk the hell out of there.

The cashier bagged the groceries and put them in the cart like she had all the time in the world. Chewing on some gum, like she was a cow with a cud. She *finally* starts scanning my purchases. No greeting or anything. Well, she probably has her own problems.

"Ma'am, that petroleum jelly is two for $4.00, not $2.75 apiece," I tell her. She pushed some buttons on her register and checked the tape. Pulling the microphone to her with her claws, she said, "Price check, H & B, price check Lane 5."

"Lady, the petroleum jelly is right there, see? Two for $4.00." I point to the *HUGE* sign just behind the checkout lane.

"I still got to wait for the price check, OK? We gone get you your *Vas-e-line*," she says rolling her eyes.

Jealous, tired heifer with that tacky weave.

She starts scanning my purchases again and I noticed, once more, that there was an error. The baby powder rang up $1.00 more than advertised. She had just picked up the ketchup when I said, "Hold up, that baby powder is not priced correctly."

13

In irritation, she slams the bottle of ketchup on the conveyor belt. The top of the ketchup bottle flies off and I watch amazed as ketchup splatters onto the front.... of....my...new...pink...suit!

I just SNAP! I'm gonna beat this stick heifer's ass. I reach over and grab a handful of that weave and pull it slap off. That cashier comes around the side of the lane and charges like a Bull Moose. Arms flailing in the air, connecting with nothing. "Catfight!" somebody yells. Just as soon as I got in a good punch, I feel arms restraining me.

"Let me go!" I shout.

"Yeah, let that punk ass fairy go!" the cashier screams.

Security holds us tight, though. They tussle with us until we are in the manager's office. The cashier was rolling her eyes and cussing up a storm. Oh, if I could just get close enough, she'd be wearing a size 12 foot up her ass for sure.

The manager walks in mopping at his forehead. He takes one look at the cashier and tells her "You're fired." The cashier cusses the manager so long and colorfully, I know right then she is the devil's spawn.

The security guard let me go after she left. He went right over to the sink and washed his hands. Really

14

scrubbed at them. Now, ketchup ain't *that* hard to get off.

"Ah, Miss....Uhm Mister...what is the problem?" The manager asks me.

I was so worked up, my voice rose two octaves, "That *heifer* splashed ketchup all over my suit. *Look at it!* I want my money for this suit. I can't *believe* this shit! I come in here, minding my own damn business and *your* cashier just jumps on me! I ought to *sue* you!"

"Calm down, Ma'am...Mister. We can settle everything here. How much is the suit worth to you?" He asks.

"Two hundred dollars. It's an *original!*" I proclaim.

"Fine," he says and counts out the money.

"Oh, and one other thing, we would appreciate if you would shop elsewhere from now on."

Now don't this beat all. Dismissed, liked I started this mess. *Jealous ass punk ass asshole!*

I muster up all the arrogance passed down from mothers to daughters and soaked up by me. I hold my head high and walk out of the office. Ignoring the snickers and whispers, I pick up my bag and put on my best butt strut and sashay the hell out of that damn store forever.

Jealous ass people. Always jealous of me.

Forget them!

LAYING ON OF THE HANDS

Fifth Street Divine United Sanctified Church of the One and Only.

The organ music swells and with it the testifying in the room increases. *Thank ya! Abadalabaya. Senuricolopolalapapabulaya. Thank ya! You've been so good to me!*

When the tenor begins his solo, the Soul Train dancers take to the aisle. They got the Homey Ghost. *Heal me! Thank ya! In your name, I claim my healing today! Abalabadouba. Thank ya!*

The preacher slowly begins praying. Will you *look* at Miss Johnson? Legs gaped wide open, offering him a front seat view to hell. I see some of the male choir singers shifting in their seats, trying to get a better view.

His low, melodious voice makes me squirm in my seat. My panties are soaked straight through. There'll probably be a wet spot when I get up. Thank goodness I wore navy. I look back at the preacher, his succulent lips moving slowly. I can just imagine them on my....what the hell am I thinking? I am in church! Focus, girl! Focus!

Here comes my favorite part—Healing Altar Prayer. I hop up out of the seat before he gets all the words out of his mouth. Damn! Miss Johnson done hopped her happy ass in front of me! What she gonna tell him, he don't already know? Everybody already heard the story—five kids, another in the oven, common-law husband walked out, she ain't got no baby-sitter, child protective services want her kids, blah, blah, blah. Hurry up!

He smacks her forehead hard! *Knock some sense into her crazy ass!* Shoot, he's probably sick and tired of hearing the same story every week. He ought to tell her that if she would just keep those legs closed at home and at church, she might be able to do better. The deacons help her to her seat. Does that deacon have his hand on her breast? Why does the other one have his hand on her butt? Oh well…...

My turn.

I confess what a sinner I am. I have boyfriend problems, money problems and Mama and Daddy problems.

He looks deep into my eyes.

I show him my soul.

I see him reaching towards my forehead. Healing me. His hand connects and the electrical impulses in my brain go haywire. Pop! Pop! Pop! The room spins and goes dark.…..

I smell something funky! I open my eyes and a Sister is blowing her must-of-been-shit-she-ate-for-lunch breath in my face. I look around and realize I'm in the pastor's study. Sister Stank Breath keeps on talking, stinking up my personal space. *Can't she smell it?* She tells me the pastor wants me to stay here until he can *personally* check on me. I nod, otherwise, I might spit up my guts all over her.

The pastor comes in and dismisses Sister Butt. Can't say I'm sorry to see her go. I wish she could take that funk with her though. He sits down next to me on the couch; asks me what is really troubling me. My "stuff" starts tingling. I feel the moisture beginning to leak. I look at him and I can't speak. Though I am speechless, my nipples rise to the occasion and speak for me. I see him look down at my chest. He asks me again what is troubling me. *Why do I have butterflies in my stomach?* I just start crying.

He reaches over and hugs me. Uhm, this feels *good*! I press my face into his shirt and inhale. Gray Flannel. Oh my goodness! I am *weak* for a man wearing Gray Flannel. I move my face up and rub my cheek against his. Whiskers! I imagine them on my nip...STOP IT! He is a *preacher*. My spiritual confidant and all.

Reluctantly, I lean back and look into those dark, inky eyes.

They pull to me.

18

I start to tell him about my boyfriend problems, my low self-esteem, my inability to leave my parent's house and how they treat me like I was twelve, not thirty. I feel *unloved.*

I pause, drained at my declarations of unworthiness.

"Sister, you need to be healed *right* now."

Heal me! Please, heal me!

"I have a special healing for someone like you."

Come with it, pastor!

"Let me tell my staff not to disturb me while I give you this special healing."

Tell 'em! Let me be healed!

He goes out into the hallway and I can hear him having a low conversation with someone. He returns in less than a minute. Walking over to the phone, he turns the ringer off.

"So we won't be interrupted," he says.

I know this healing is going to be good. I can feel it in the air already. He walks back over to the couch and asks me to lie on my stomach. He tells me a good healing always starts with release of tension—a massage. I hear him fumbling in a desk drawer then he pulls out a bottle of yellow liquid.

What the f....?

"Healing oil, Sister. I massage only with healing oil."

19

I relax back into the couch. At the first touch, my butt muscles clench. He moves his hands around my neck in a slow, circular motion. *Is it getting hot in here or is it me?*

"Remove the blouse."

For what?

"The oil will stain the blouse."

Oh.

I remove the blouse. It is just my bad luck I had on my new transparent bra. He looks down at my nipples and my nipples look right back at him. I lay back down on my stomach. He rubs some oil in his palms, blows on them and starts to rub my shoulders. Damn! That holy oil is *hot*! The breath whooshes out of me. I sink lower into the couch as his hands move lower down my back. He begins praying for me to feel loved.

"Turn over."

Already? I was just getting into the back massage.

I flip over and close my eyes. He starts rubbing my neck and slowly moves down to the tops of my breasts. He picks up the bottle of oil. Oho! He spilt a good bit across my chest. I look around for some Kleenex or paper towels, but I don't see anything.

"Just remove the bra so the oil won't mess it all up."

I freeze. *Now what kind of healing is this preacher trying to do?*

"One of the worse things man has done to his precious helpmate, is to demoralize her femininity. I rejoice in all womanhood. I am not ashamed of *my* body and neither should you. Your breasts are the givers of nourishment. I come in my master's name to heal you of your shame!" he implores. "If you feel uncomfortable, I'll remove my shirt also."

I do remember all the hateful things my ignorant boyfriend said about my body. Itty-bitty. My Mama always telling me to put tissue in my bra, because a man wants to see some curves and all. Giving me a push-up brassiere for my birthday.

I rip that bra off!

The pastor rushes over and begins to massage my breasts. He is praying loudly. Praying that I will feel love and receive love when it is offered. He must have prayed five minutes. When he finishes, he says he needs to kiss my breasts so that they will know love.

At this point, the healing is working. I am really starting to feel love. I tell him to go ahead. He kisses the tops, then the sides of my breasts. I see him opening his mouth to kiss my nipple.

Must be a French kiss. Yes! Yes! I feel the love. I am getting *healed!*

His kiss moves to my stomach. I feel his tongue in my navel.

Oooh yes.

His head moves down to the waistband of my skirt. Still licking and kissing. He begins to massage my upper thighs. Suddenly, he stops.

What?

"Remove your pantyhose so the oil won't stain them."

I pull that skirt high and shimmy out of those pantyhose in a flash. He resumes massaging my thighs, his hands moving higher and higher until they brush against my wet panties.

Heal me.

"Now, Sister, I want you to remove your skirt. All of you must receive the holy oil in order to get *complete* healing."

Now that makes sense don't it?

I stand up and drop the skirt, revealing the transparent panties to match the bra. I lay back down ready for my healing to continue.

"I need to be dressed as you are to continue the healing. I want you to see and feel my love." I watch as he gets out of his pants, his back to me. He returns to the couch, grabs my hand and places it on his crotch.

"*Feel* the love I have for you Sister!"

It's *BIG* love. I feel the healing power all over me. My breasts are aching, my "stuff" is dripping and my toes are curling. Healing me.

He leans over and kisses me on the mouth. "A kiss of salvation," he says.

He will save me from feeling unloved by the world.

I feel him push my panties to the side, but I don't care. I *need* healing. He pushes into me. I try to get up. He holds onto my shoulders and begins thrusting and praying for me to receive *all* the *love* he has to give. He prays this over and over and over again. I think I start to pray with him.

Suddenly he stands. A hot liquid gushes onto my breasts, runs down my stomach.

"My love!" he says and begins rubbing the liquid into my breasts and belly.

I am out of control. I shout out in a strange language. *Ahayabilaya! Thank ya! Heratobibolamaya! Thank ya! I feel the love! Thank ya! Thank ya!*

I finally come down off my "healing" high. I know something amazing has occurred here. This man is *truly* a miracle worker.

He kisses me and helps me dress.

"Woman, thou art healed," he says.

I walk out into the hallway, floating on a cloud. I pass the deacon. He has a smirk on his face.

"Brother, I am *healed*!" I shout. I hear him snicker, but I keep on walking. I tell the church secretary I want to join the choir, the usher board and the missionary committee. I have been healed!

She looks at me, with a knowing grin on her face, "I know," she says, "the pastor must have done some 'laying of the hands' on you."

How did she know?

"That's right. I received love and I am now worthy to give love," I tell her proudly.

"Well, that's good and all, but don't let the pastor's wife hear about your 'special healing' session," she whispers and winks. I hear them laughing as I leave.

I walk out of that church excited. I need to "heal" someone else. Spread the good news. Testify to somebody of the goodness of "healing" love. I talk to everybody I know. Some of them laugh in my face, but a lot of them let me "heal" them too. They said they didn't know I could "heal" like that.

My Mama and Daddy called and told me to quit "healing" everybody. Folks are gonna talk. So what? I don't care what they say. They can't tell it like I can tell it. I was there! I am a living testimony of the healing salvation delivered through my pastor. He awakened my dead love and set me free!

Think what you want, but all I *do* know is that you ain't been "healed" until my pastor lays his hands on you! Don't let the Street Committee sway you!

Thank ya! Jobolamiyabolabaya!

MASSAGE-A-TWA...

Ménage à trois.
Every man's fantasy.
Two women, one man.

My husband asked me if I would have a ménage á trois. He said it so casually, as if it was no big deal. Like he was asking me to pick up his dry-cleaning on the way home. He smiles when he tells me to think about it. It will spice up things, he says, before picking up his briefcase and walking outside to his car just as casual as you please. As if the request from him to screw another woman, *in my face*, would in no way offend me. My participation would, in fact, lessen his sin.

I feel the scar as it puckers up on my brain. Cells permanently rendered useless by this request. Forever etched in my mind, that the *man* I married and gave my heart, soul and body to wants a ménage á trois. Thinks it's a great idea.

BASTARD! I kick over a chair and fling clothes around the room. *FUCKING, IGNORANT, BASTARD*! Who the *fuck* does he think he is? He, me and she. The pain slices through me like an unshielded laser.

Massage a twat.

26

That's what I'd call it 'cause that's what it really is. The need for a man to massage a twat or two that he's not use to.

Is he saying my pussy ain't enough? Is that what this prince-to-prick I married is telling me? Hell, yes, that's what he is saying. If I go along once, he's gonna want it again and again and again. That two-legged snake. I ought to go down to his job and *slap* the teeth out of his mouth.

WHAAM! I slam a chair into the wall, leaving four leg holes. Perverted *S.O.B.*! I howl with the pain from that one solitary, stupid request. The tears fall down my face, snot runs out of my nose, spit bubbles on my lips. I age a decade in seconds.

SMASH!

Seven years bad luck.

WHO GIVES A *FUCK*?!

The initial pain and shock gradually subsides, leaving me as deflated as a new inner tube.

Why? Why all of a sudden this *shit*? We are *married*, not dating. This is some shit you try out in college or at least before you say "I do". You don't *keep* doing it!

Where did this come from?

Deep down, I already know. It's always been there. His "in the closet" fantasy. His punk-ass was just afraid to say it. Must be feeling pretty comfortable to ask now.

Thinks he *knows* me. Thinks he knows how I will react. BASTARD! I will not knowingly share *anybody's* Johnson!

Massage a twat. Who started this shit? Did it start with cavemen and just continue throughout the ages? Or did some oversexed mofo' invent the idea? Made a couple of women think it was a great idea to service him together. He gets off and they are left frustrated. Hell, it's hard for one man to handle one woman who knows her way around the bed, much less two. Somebody's gonna come up short.

My mind reels with a bazillion questions:

How in the hell is this *thing* supposed to be good for a marriage?

How long has he been *thinking* about this shit?

What if he enjoys screwing *her* more than *me*?

What if he does things with *her*, he has *never* done with me?

Who did he do them with?

Who gets firsts?

Will she try to touch *me*?

Will he try to get *me* to touch *her*?

Will I be able to handle his fucking *somebody else*?

Will he want to fuck her without *me* around?

Who is this bitch?

What is she? Hetero? Bi? Tri?

Where has her pussy been before?

Why is he in a goddamn hurry to get *up* in there?

Has he been there *before*?

Am I *already* sleeping with this woman?!

SPICE MY ASS!

It's the magazines, I'm thinking. The pornographic magazines and tapes he collects like a pension check each month. I always feared that that mess would seep into his brain and make him want more...different... what he didn't have.

Massage a twat? Look at the magazines! *See it*! They lock like they are really enjoying it. The man always looks like a king in his castle—laid flat on his back while women lick, suck, nibble and ride. Minimum output, maximum input. I wonder if these silly women are trying to outdo the other. You know, my pussy is better than her pussy.

I look at the disheveled room. Clothes flung about, holes in the wall. Just like my hopes and dreams—ripping at my soul like old wallpaper. This isn't what I thought marriage would be about.

I'm going to call a locksmith, pack the fuckers' things and set them outside the door. Better yet, I ought to bleach all his clothes and shoes, take my shit and scat. Hell. I'll *exhale* and set all his shit on fire!

I take a deep breath, feeling a need to revenge this trespass on my psyche. The devaluation of my being biting at my ass. I pace back and forth like a wounded, caged lioness.

Pace. Moan. Pace. Mutter. Pace. Punch the air. Pace.

My mind is all over the place.

POOWWW!

The devil on my right shoulder just slapped the hell out of the angel on my left.

Pay Back Time Sweetie.

Wanna play? Let's play.

I set the damn rules though. I choose the who and the what, he can choose the where. Probably here, knowing his deceitful ass.

Who will it be? Hmmmm. Definitely someone tall, thick and coloring doesn't matter.

I get firsts and I decide what we do together.

Toys are acceptable.

Recent, negative STD test in hand at the door.

Condoms and dental dams a must.

No means no.

Stop means stop.

NO stimulants! Use what you got or get the *fuck* out the door!

Now, who the hell do I know that would be willing to participate in this freaky crap? I scan the list of unusual suspects in my mind bank first.

What is the name of that chick that they were calling a freak at the office just last week? Shit, I wish I'd paid more attention to those loose lips.

I know someone was caught screwing in the copy room. But damn, that was a year ago…

Surely, I must have an *acquaintance* that I can ask to participate that won't cuss me out or spread my "request" around? Won't think I'm crazy or a fool or a freak? Won't try to work their own "private" deal on the side?

Who will it be?!

Stumbling about the recesses of my brain—opening old closet doors and welding shut others. Sliding the curtain to the side…a feeling of sunlight on my face…realization jockeying with sudden confirmation in my gut.

I…know…who…to…ask.

So obvious, right in my face the whole time.

I call. Scared, shivering, pissed. So many "what ifs" hang in the air.

I ask. I just blurt it out.

The answer is …yes. Yes! Relief is felt down to the hangnails on my toes.

Tonight around seven o'clock? Yes.

31

Pay back is mine, saith this wife!

I call my husband and relay what I have just set up. He just about fell-the-fuck out. He said he felt that I may have been *offended* by his request this morning. He's glad to see I'm willing to spice up our lovelife and experiment.

He arrives home two hours early to "prepare." Anxious for my *friend* to get here. Anxious to be up in another twat. Just wants to get his Johnson wet. *Pussysnatcher!*

The doorbell rings.

I assure him I'll get it. He is so hyped, he is practically jumping up and down. I look through the peephole. Yep, right on time. My husband is breathing on the back of my neck, anticipating a fuckfest to the nth degree. *Massage a twat* time.

He helps me open the door to...Brian, my ex-husband.

Brian smiles. Looks at me with eyes already smoldering with remembrances of my pussy.

He, me, and he. Ménage à trois.

My husband looks confused, not sure why he is here, what is going on, then... sudden clarity. Fury etches his eyes, chisels his face. How could I do this? What the hell is wrong with *me*?! How long has *this shit* been going on? Me fucking Brian with *him* watching?! Participating? I must have lost my damn mind! Damn

32

freak! Slamming the bedroom door, clicking the lock in place.

Like I really want to go in there. To that killer of self-esteem; demoralizer of femininity.

I pick my keys...my suitcase is already in the car...walk into the night.

Massage a twat.
Every man's fantasy.
Two women, one man.
Ménage á trois.
Equal Opportunity.

AND THE DRAMA GOES ON...

"Hello?"

Silence greets me.

"Hello?" I say again.

"Yes, is this 555-8786?" A woman asks.

"Yes, it is."

"Ugh, who is this?" She asks.

What? Where is the phone etiquette here? "I believe the correct question is 'May I speak to whoever it is you are trying to reach.' "

"Well, I'm *trying* to reach whoever is at this damn number," she snaps.

"Hold up. Who, exactly, is it that you are trying to get?" I asked perturbed. This conversation has gone on longer that I wanted it to.

"Look, *heffa*, I found this number in my husband's pants pocket and I want to know whose it is," the woman says nastily.

"And?" I ask.

"And I want to know why he's got your number in his pants pocket!"

"Who *is* your man anyway?" I ask exasperated.

"Who did you give your number to?"

"Look, lady, I really don't need this shit. So maybe *you* should ask whoever how they got this number."

"No, *you look*, bitch. I want to know *why* my husband has this damn number and *who* the hell you are!" She yelled in the phone.

"Who the *fuck* you calling a *bitch*?! Now I don't have a flying fuck about who the hell your man, husband or whatever is. But I do know your funky ass don't need to call my house again!"

BLAM! I slammed that phone down hard enough to break her eardrums.

RRRIIIINNNNGGG!

"Hello!"

"I *know* you didn't hang the phone up on me. I just *know* you didn't!" the same woman says.

"Hell, yes, I did!"

"It's *obvious* to me that you and my husband have something going on," she continued.

"It's obvious to *me* that you don't know what the hell you are talking about!"

"You slut! Get your...

"Fuck you!"

"...own damn man!"

"Are you married?

"Yes."

"Is he still there?"

"Yes."

"Then why you calling me? Seems like if you really wanted to know something, you could ask the person right there in your damn face!"

"I'm asking *you*, heffa."

"Who the *fuck* you think you are talking to? You ain't running *nothing*, and I mean *nada* over here. You might be running some shit over there, but not over here, chick."

"I'm gonna get to the bottom of this shit and when I do, I'm gonna...beat...your...ass."

"Bring it on, you trifling *bitch*! You can't do *shit* to me, I can't do to you. Fuck you! Don't call here again!"

BLAM! Stupid ass woman!

Here I am minding my own business and I get this. Every time a woman finds a number in a pocket or checks the caller ID, she gets suspicious. Damn! Ask your man about the number if you didn't dial it! Do they do that? *No*! They immediately assume the worse. And you know what they say about assumptions—it's the mother of all fuckups.

When a woman decides to call another woman about her "man", she is just laying down the foundation for self-denial, looking for every damn reason, but the obvious one.

Why are you calling another woman's house any damn way? If you are married, ask him. If you are

36

separated or divorce, it doesn't matter. And if you are dating, that shit doesn't even count.

Face it. You don't even really *want* to know. You just want an excuse. Any damn one will do. 'She works with him. She probably bought something from him. She needed him as a reference.' Any damn thing. To admit that he wrote the number down to try to get a "hookup" with another woman, is a slap in the face. It couldn't have been his idea. Right? 'She forced him to take her number. He was just being polite. He meant to throw it away and forgot.' Yeah.

Now you, the "real" woman in this situation, decide to go into "Jerry Springer" mode. Call up the other woman and warn her off or there will be trouble. More trouble than this other woman wants, you hope.

Ladies, you need to *cut this shit out!*

If you are suspicious, what you need to do is first, do your homework, then secondly, pin his ass to the wall. Good evidence starts with a *full* personal investigation. Go through *every* piece of clothes he owns, including the shorts. Search every nook and cranny in the house. Wait until he is asleep and toss the car. Determine if your *suspicions* are real. Then, you just start spitting out the questions and see if his answers match yours.

Who is she?

Where do you know her from?

How did you get her number?

Did she volunteer it or did you ask for it?

Why did you need the number?

Have you called the number?

Where else have you seen her?

Where were you last Friday night when you said you had to work late and nobody answered the phone?

What about last week when you were late getting back from lunch?

Who'd you have lunch with?

Where did you run into her again?

Don't let his ass go to the bathroom, get a drink or a cigarette. Stick to his ass like glue. Then, and only then will you know if he is legit or trying to run a game here.

And if he's *not* legit what are you gonna do? Cry? Keep your hurt feelings inside, while he begs for your forgiveness? Walk around mopey and depressed? Probably.

Why don't you cuss him out? Scared he'll leave? So what if he does? One won't, a thousand will. What the heck are you losing? He's already giving up the dick. There ain't a man alive that will admit to why he really has the number if he was trying to get a hookup. It will never, ever be his fault.

So why you asking? I say either *do something* or *shut the hell up* about it! Slap him. Punch him. Put his ass

38

out. *Do not* harass the other woman. You ain't sleeping with her, you sleeping with him. *She* didn't promise to love, honor and be faithful. *He* did. *She* ain't calling him. *He's* calling her.

Now your scare tactics have worked. He's not in contact with her anymore, so he says. He seems remorseful. Where are you at? Nervous all the time. Calling him fifty times a day at work, trying to account for every minute he's not with you. Still checking out the clothes, knowing you ain't gonna find shit, since he is onto your ass.

You got what you wanted didn't you? He's here and she's there...but it won't ever be the same now that you realize that your pussy can be replaced.

Floozy.

Slut.

Homewrecker.

The Other Woman.

Call them what you want. They've probably have heard it before. They ain't going away. All you can do is realize that a man might be a dog, but a woman can be a bitch, too.

Woof!

THE PROOF IS IN THE PUDDING

Man, I just can't believe this mess!

Here I am in a place I never thought I would see the inside of— prison.

Another statistic.

But damn, I didn't do the crime! Yeah, I guess you're saying you heard that before, but it's true. I wasn't framed or anything. The evidence pointed to me, *but I didn't do it!*

See, it was a case of stupid choices. Stupid *pudding* choices. Yeah, I said pudding. You know coochie, poontang, cuda, cookie—what women got between their legs. I'm not the first man to ride the Concorde to Hell by using the wrong head. By no means am I saying that women are evil. They just have what any red-blooded man wants and sometimes do stupid things to get.

Ten to twenty-five for ignorance. I want to blame somebody, anybody. Six months ago, I was living large and in charge. Had a wife and two kids...why did I go and mess it up like this?

Another fucked up life in a fucked up world.

My wife just sent over the divorce paper with my lawyer.

SHIT! SHIT! SHIT!

I punched the wall and watched the blood drip from my knuckles. God, I need some help here.

Another chance. Anything but this damn box to call home.

ANYTHING....

I considered myself a never-to-be-reformed-until-caught, undercover womanizer. Variety *is* the spice of life and variety comes in all colors, shapes, sizes and skills.

Stop tripping! This is America. Girls give up pudding like you asked for a glass of ice water. Shit, women have been slapping their pudding in my face and on my lap since I was in grade school. I had my "playa" card in the eighth grade.

I turned in my card for good (so I thought) when I met my future wife. Boy, she set me on my ass. Ignored a brother, laughed in my face and cut my conversations very, very short. For a change, I was panting after a woman like a dog trying to get a bone. Neglected all my other honeys until I had no other honeys. I wanted her something *bad!* I pursued her and wooed until she finally agreed to date me. And when she finally gave up the drawers after nine months of begging, I knew this was THE ONE. I married her the next year.

Then things just . . .changed. I don't mean overnight, but gradually. Sexy lingerie became a bad word. Hell!

Sex became a bad word. And her mother...how can I say this nicely? Her mother wouldn't take her tail home. I mean damn near everyday I got home, there is my mother-in-law sitting in *my* favorite chair watching our television. She wasn't in a rush to go home either. After awhile, I was staying later and later at the office, going by the bar to relax before I went home. *What the hell was I going home for*?

The ladies tried to serve it up to me right from the start. Women can tell when you're having home trouble. They smell the blood and go for the kill. They are *not* the weaker sex, just a slicker predator. I tried and tried to resist all the trite come-ons and sly looks. But damn, the more I resisted, the more pudding was wiggled past my face. At first, I was like a great oak tree—true, solid and unyielding, then along came Trish.

Trish was a twenty-something law student with looks. Trouble with an upper class "T". I got so tongue-tied when she first spoke to me, I know she thought I was mentally-challenged. But we just clicked—karma to karma, psyche to psyche. That oak tree shrunk to fit inside my pants. Messed me *all* the way up.

Boy, that Trish turned me onto some freaky shit— bondage, S&M, handcuffs, riding the Milky Way, playacting— that girl had skills and some! If I had a fantasy, she had a better one. I had my cake and was eating that sucker in one gulp. Man, it was hard going home and not trying that shit out on my wife. If I had, she would have tripped me *straight* out the door!

See, my wife can be quite straight-laced and uptight. You *do not* deviate from basic sexual routines. There *is* no such word as kinky in her vocabulary. Experimentation is *not* good in her book.

Now you can imagine my constant frustration! I had to work it off somewhere, didn't I? Trish *loved* me frustrated, carrying a load of pent-up anger. The more I slapped it, tweaked it and nipped it, the hotter she became. *The pudding was strong and I couldn't go wrong!*

Trish and I kicked it six glorious months. Months when I started to reconsider the marriage thing altogether. Then, I received the big news—my wife was pregnant.

Pissed me the hell *off*!

How in the heck could that have happened? I mean, dag, I might get some twice a month.

That shit swiveled my head like that girl on the *Exorcist* and I told Trish we were over. I hated to see her go, but I couldn't be out there messing around and have a pregnant wife, now could I?

Things were back to normal (in my mind anyway) in a snap. No more working late or barhopping after work. One thing that didn't change was my mother-in-law being at the house every day. I walked in on her telling my wife that she was a fool for having a child with a man like me. What exactly did she *think* I was doing until 10 or 11 o'clock at night? I slammed the door and she immediately stopped talking. Entering the living room, I saw my wife looking like she wanted to cry and her mother rolling her eyes. I knew that my little shred of happiness was just about to go on hiatus again. Oh well...

I slipped back into my old habits fast. A string of short affairs—Liz, Tamia, Katie, Terry, Velma, Nadia, Serena, Yolanda, and so on. I forget all their names and I didn't keep no *damn black book*! I wanted to get laid and laid I got. Don't get me wrong, I wasn't hitting up anything in a skirt, I was "selective". It's just that a lot of women passed my "selectivity" test.

My son was born and before you could blink, my wife was pregnant again. But I couldn't stop my roll at that point anyway. Truth be told, I just didn't want to.

Then guess who I stumbled upon again? Yes, Trish, looking finer than ever. Man I was back in the saddle again! Girlfriend had learned some new tricks and I was a willing subject. *Hello!*

One night, after a particularly long "workout," I dragged my ass home and collapsed in bed. No shower or nothing. I guess I wanted my wife to know. Shit, I *had* options. She could take me or leave me. Well, Trish was

44

killed that night. I didn't find out until two days later. She had missed our date so I called her apartment and a man answered. He identified himself as a policeman and asked me who I was. I broke out in a sweat and hung up.

I went to the library at lunch and found the article concerning her death. No, that isn't correct. Trish was murdered. Strangled. They thought it was kinky sex gone bad— sexual asphyxiation.

Damn! Damn! Damn!

A police officer was waiting to talk to me at the office when I returned from lunch. They'd traced the number I called from and they had some questions.

How did you know Trish? *Just in passing.*

Why did you call? *I had some questions concerning a private matter.*

Were you involved? *NO!* Calm down. Calm down.

So you are saying you were not intimately involved with the murdered lady? *Yes, that's exactly what I am saying.*

Have you ever been to her apartment? *No.*

Never? *No.*

The doorman saw a man leaving her apartment that night. Was it you? *Like I said I have never been to Trish's apartment.*

Would you submit to a blood test? *For what?*

To rule you out as a suspect, of course. *Are you suspecting every man she knows?*

Pretty much.

I agreed to the test. Hell, Trish was alive and well when I left her. I didn't expect them to find any trace of my having been there.

One week later, the same police officer showed up at my house on a Sunday morning to arrest me for the murder of Trish. And the rest, as they say, is history.

DNA indicated that the semen found in her pudding, was 99.7% compatible with me. See, Trish and I didn't use condoms. She had negative STD tests and so did I. On that particular night, we had a S & M feast. She liked it rough and I got rough like she liked it. *But I didn't kill her.*

The prosecution's case stated that she was tied up, brutally raped, sodomized and strangled. Since I lied about knowing her intimately, my credibility was shot and the DNA test slammed the door on my fate.

So here I am.....

Ten to twenty-five. Wasting time. Ruined life. A convicted felon.

Because of the proof that was found in her pudding.

I might be an adulterer, but I am no murderer!

Right.

But who cares?!

Mooooooooo Cow

Let me hip you before the goose pecks you again.

I see so many of my sisters out there lying to themselves, paddling down the river Denial with one broke-ass oar. Miserable because they have one, two, six kids and no husband. Don't get me wrong, they are living with their babies' daddy. He just won't marry them. And they want to be married. Bad.

What, exactly, is his motivation to get married? Check this out. Would you pay for fruit if you had all the fruit trees in your back yard? Would you buy a new car, if somebody was giving you one free? Would you buy a house, if your folks gave you one? Would you buy clothes if you owned the store? Soooooooooo, why would any man buy the *cow*, when the *milk* is free?

Yes, I said free. I mean you cook for him, clean for him, have children with him, split the bills with him and have regular sex with him. All without marriage. What more can he want?

Oh, and the lies you tell yourself:

Everybody is doing it so it must be all right. *How many happy families you seen shacking?*

We want to get to know each other better and see if we are compatible. *I could be wrong, but I thought that was what dating was for.*

We can save money for marriage. *Have you heard the term budget?*

He won't leave me if I have a child. *Did you miss the statistics?*

Biggest Lie. He will marry me eventually.

Girl, please! If you are going to lie to somebody, don't let it be you! Like they say, if you put the cart before the horse, you aren't going anywhere. You'll be stuck in the same broke-down spot, until the end.

You will cohabitant five, ten or more years, then you catch him cheating. *Now I know you ain't really surprised are you?* You put him out. *You* keep the kids, the stretch marks from those kids, the house you can't afford on one salary, all the bills that go along with that house you can't afford and he gets off. He's happy as hell—now he can save money not having to get a hotel room. You can't get half, 'cause you're not married, remember? All you'll be is mad.

Why did you have children and you weren't married? I know. You got caught up in the moment and it just happened.

Bullshit!

You didn't get pregnant all the time you were dating. You move in together and BOOM, pregnant. And unmarried.

Oh, he asked you to have a baby. I see. If he had asked me, I would have jumped up right then, excited because I *know* he's got a ring somewhere close by. We are getting married! Soon! See, I don't rent out the uterus and I ain't gonna be no surrogate mother for *nobody's* children.

And for heaven's sake, don't let him die! Your name can't be found on *shit*! His mom's name is on his life insurance policy. Your name isn't on the deed to the house, so his folks get it. That car you been paying on together ain't got your name nowhere near the title. And you *know* he don't have a will. You won't have jack shit. Oh, they'll let you pay for the funeral, but after that, sister you gots to go.

His folks love you? Are you *slow* or something? Money makes folks act a *fool*! They will put you and your kids out on the street before the flowers bloom on his grave. You'll be taking the bus to work.

Share the money? Girl, you must be tripping. He left that money to his Moma because that's must be who he wanted to have it. And she will tell you so. Ask her for some if you don't believe me. I'm *telling* you!

49

I know you thought you had reached the level of "wifedom" in their eyes. After all, y'all been together all those years. Not! You were his "friend." Period. His family will act like they don't know you that well at all. Get to stepping!

Look at yourself. You've invested time, hard-earned money and your body in this "shacking up" relationship and you could end up with zilch! Nada! Why are you continuing to remain at this level? When are you going to wake the fuck up?!

I mean, how long can you *date* somebody? I give them two years, after that, I already know I ain't "The One" for him. If I was, he would have asked me to marry him.

Live together? No way. A roommate can split the bills just as well as I can.

Children? Not without marriage. You ain't gonna walk out one day without me getting my half.

Buying stuff together and my name isn't listed as co-owner or something? Not while I am breathing.

Sisters, you can either control your life or your life will control you. Be proactive, not reactive. Don't believe the hype! Believe me when I say, *make his ass buy the cow before he gets the milk!*

THE JANITOR

Clean up woman

She's tough-uh-uhhhhhhh, I mean she really cleans uppppp!

Clean up woman. Boy, was that song ever true. I'm just like the clean up woman, except I'm a man, so I call myself a janitor. And this janitor gets *a lot* of bizness. You think I'm kidding don't you? Well, my "janitorial business" pays for my house, my BMW, my snappy clothes *and* I have money left over to spare.

Naw, I'm not no pimp or gigolo. I'm your everyday run-of-the mill brother. My looks are aw'ight, but nothing special.

So how do I do this? Shoot, it's just too easy. There are millions and I mean *millions* of women out there, unfulfilled and looking for a brother just like me. So why shouldn't I capitalize while I fulfill the needs of the marketplace?

Like any other entrepreneur, I made mistakes when I first started my "business." I made bad selections in my "clients", had high turnover, chose poor meeting places and had a lot of account receivables. Basically, these low class women used me, abused me and wanted every thing on credit. And of course, they NEVER paid their bills.

This jacked up my cash flow. Bad. I couldn't keep a car or an apartment because my payments were always behind, because my "clients" didn't pay me like they were supposed to. They said they had their own bills, their husbands would miss the money, etc. Anyway, they didn't pay me. I was *struggling*. Had to hustle up a job here and there just to feed myself. Man, I was in a sorry state.

One day, I just had a talk with myself about the state of the "business"—no money, no car, no apartment and food sometimes. Things just had to change. I wrote out a new "business plan" which I was determined to follow. I gave myself six months to get established. After that, I guessed I was going to have to put in an application at Sears. I borrowed $300 dollars from my cousin, had some *foine* business cards printed up, bought a new suit and tried the business again. Here's the basics of the plan:

The Business Plan

Owner: Myself

Type of Business: Personal Janitorial Services

Type of Company: Sole Proprietorship

Bylaws:

1.   Meet women at upscale places, such as museums, high price boutiques, charity luncheons, golf courses, and spas.

    a.   Preferences given to much younger wives of much older spouses.

    b.   Preferences given to young widows of much older spouses;

2.   Choose clients based solely upon their own or their spouses income;

3.   Verify residence address. Must be an upscale neighborhood. Preferences given to those that have the means and need to employ a maid, gardener, au pair and/or a pool person;

4.   Verify the existence of a Platinum Visa/Mastercard or a American Express Blue card;

5.   Janitorial services are paid for at the time that services are rendered. Gifts above the service price are graciously accepted;

6.   Payment for services is NOT refundable.

    a.   We aim to please, therefore, in the event that the "client" is displeased in any way, we will REDO the job once for free.

    b.   Repeated complaints by "client" will effectively void any future service request;

7.   All lodging and meals will be paid for by the "client";

8.   The client will indemnify and hold blameless the janitorial service in the event of domestic disturbances arising from the use of the services we provide;

9.   All visits will be prearranged and agreed upon prior to the meeting date.

   a.   There will be NO unannounced visits to the Janitorial Service headquarters for any reason.

   b.   Contact for services from the Janitorial Service will be made via pager to 555-6969;

10. I will be impeccably groomed at all times—neat haircut, freshly laundered clothes, understated cologne, no scuffed shoes;

11. I will always be tactful;

12. I will always be on time; and

13. The "client" is always right.

Cost of Services (Mix and Match)

1.	Basic Sex/hour	$300.00
2.	Cunnilingus	$200.00
3.	Reciprocal Fellatio	Gratis
4.	Milky Way	$200.00
5.	S&M/Bondage	$500.00
6.	Playacting	$200.00
7.	Toe-Sucking	$100.00
8.	Massage	Gratis

Cash Flow Projections (Year 1)

	Estimated Clients	Avg. Monthly Visits	Avg.Client Transaction	Monthly Income	Annual Income
Jan	1	4	500	2000	2,000
Feb	3	12	500	6000	8,000
March	4	16	550	8000	16,000
April	5	20	550	11K	27,000
May	6	24	600	14.4K	41,400
June	7	28	600	16.8K	58,200
July	8	32	600	19.2K	77,400
Aug	9	36	600	21.6K	99,000
Sept	10	40	600	24K	123,000
Oct	10	40	600	24K	147,000
Nov	10	40	600	24K	171,000
Dec	10	40	600	24K	195,000

Now the first month was kind of slow. I met the first victim, uh "client", at a museum, where I had been scoping her out for a week. She arrived every day at the same time and looked at the same old dry ass whack paintings. *But*, she had a fat diamond on her hand and her clothes were top notch. She shouted *LONELY*!

I positioned myself next to the painting she was always staring at— some crap that looked like the artist slit somebody's throat and let the spray fly all over the canvas. She arrived on schedule. *A lonely woman don't let you down*!

I let her stare at it for about five minutes before I made my move. I told her some trite shit about how it was one of my favorites. It was filled with deep emotions like I was and all.

55

That got her to talking and talking and talking. She seemed to think we were having a great one-sided conversation, so I suggested we continue it at a local deli, D'Cat's Meow.

It turns out that the chick was married to a state Supreme Court judge. The second "trophy" wife. He was twenty-five years older, didn't want kids, and didn't want her to work, but all he did was work. They had just bought a house up in Shaker Heights, the new enclave for the ultra-rich. She was bo-o-ored to death. Pay dirt!

I decided to take a chance. Hell, what did I have to lose? If she said yes, I might make some ducats. If she said no, we would just part and I wouldn't go to that damn museum again. I waited until she took a breath from her soliloquy and then I explained my discreet "janitorial" business. Then I waited.

She seemed to think about it, shook her head, pondered some more eons, then said, "What the hell. I'll give you a shot." I about fell out of my damn chair, but I covered it well. *I had to act like I had done this before!*

She suggested the LaHyacinth Hotel. Boy, we in high cotton now! The LaHyacinth is where my daddy used to be a maintenance man. The rooms *start* at $250 a night. I let her set up the arrangements on her, you guessed it, American Express Blue card. She's all right with me.

Did your boy *perform*? *Did* he *perform*?!

56

Let me tell you, no plumber in the world laid pipe like I did that day! *And* she paid me *cash*. I didn't have to remind her or nothing! A new businessman is born.

After two more meetings, I felt that I had laid down a "sturdy" foundation. I told her I wanted to branch out, take my business to another level. If she knew of any other friends that could use my "services," I really couldn't tell her in words the extent of my gratitude. I would have to express it. Naked.

She told two of her "closest" friends, they told somebody, and the word was out! Those women were after me like I was the original Gold Pole man. I had to *turn down* business. Really!

Who would have guessed a man like me, would become the successful businessman I am today from "janitorial services"? Fellas, "janitorial services" are in demand! Tight ass clients, great hours, pleasure-filled working environment and when you're off, you are off.

Well, as you can guess, I met all projections and then some. Need I say more?

THE NOTIFICATION

Today is my day off and I am glad for the rest. I'm also glad my child's at school and my husband's at work. I tell you, last week they worked us like Hitler himself owned the company.

I think I'll just lay here in bed all day. Forget about everything. Ignore life…let me quit. I have to get up and get my behind in gear. I've got a hundred things to do and not enough time to get them all done today. I glance once more at the pillow and push myself out of the bed and head towards the kitchen.

Ummm, the mail's here. Let me see who knows I owe them this month. Discover card. Gas bill. MasterCharge. Junk. American Express. Electricity bill. Letter from Social Services. Check from work. Tuition. Junk. Junk. Junk.

I open the check first. *Gotta make sure they didn't short my hours this week.* I can be very "colored" if you mess with my money. Good, it looks right this time. Let's see. I look at all the credit card mail with trepidation. I shift them to the side since I already know what's in them. Okay, then. Social Services. It's addressed to my husband. Probably telling him how much he'll have for retirement or something.

I turned to put the mail on the counter. The corner of the Social Services letter caught on the edge and ripped partially open. NOTIFICATION OF CHILD SUPPORT ENFORCEMENT ACTIONS it said at the top of the letter. Let me see what this mess is about…

NOTIFICATION OF CHILD SUPPORT ENFORCEMENT ACTIONS

RE: Shawn Morrison, child born to Lisa Morrison, May 4, 2001.

You have been named as the father of the above referenced child. Please contact this office immediately to arrange a paternity test. Failure to do so will result in child support enforcement actions resulting in the automatic reduction of your monthly pay in the amount of 25%.

Loss of current employment will not relieve of your child support obligations. However, child support will be reduced according to your income. In case of unemployment, your spouse's income will be enforced against.

Please contact this office at 555-7789 to arrange testing in this matter.

Sincerely,

Social Services

What?! I look at the front of the letter again. Yep, it's addressed to my husband all right. I feel the blood draining down to my feet. My chest tightens painfully. I can barely breathe. I feel dizzy, nauseous. I collapse onto the chair and plop my head on the table. I take small sips of air like I'm in the gas chamber.

Ohmigod.

Sip. Sip. Sip.

I can't believe this shit here.

Sip. Sip. Sip.

The phone rings. I ignore it. It continues to ring.

Brrrrrrrriiiiinnnnnggg. Brrrrrriiiiiinnnnnnggggg.

Sip. Sip. Sip.

Brrrrrriiiiinnnnggggg. Pick up, damn answering machine!

Sip. Sip. Sip.

Brrrrriiiiinnnnnnggggg. I pick up the phone and slam it back down. I don't give a *damn* about who it is.

I dial his cell phone. Off.

That *motherfucker*! I ain't going to have this *shit*! Hell naw! Let me get some clothes on because his ass is going to tell me something. I ain't got time for this bullshit. I have spent eleven *good years* on his ass and he does something like this? If his ass was gonna cheat, you'd think his *dumb ass* would use protection wouldn't you? No, instead he exposes me to some disease or something his trick might have. I'll fix his train.

I throw on some wrinkled pants and the shirt I had on yesterday. *Forget the ketchup stain!* I don't comb my hair, brush my teeth or wash my face in my hurry to get out the door. Trying to get to my *husband.* I back the car out and almost hit my elderly neighbor walking her dog. I wave and floor the pedal.

Thinks I'm a fool does he? I'll show him what a fool looks like. I pass the slowass drivers out sight-seeing while my life is going down the tubes. *Is that road construction?* I see a clear street and turn down it. Doesn't matter that it's a one-way street and I'm going the wrong way.

I reach his office in Guinness record time. Storming right in, I ignore the receptionist and head for his office door. He isn't there.

I march back to the receptionist, slap my hand on the desk, get in her face and ask for him. She backs up, fans the air in front of her face, looks me up and down, but doesn't say a word. I ask her where he is again. Still fanning the air, she tells me he's at a site clear across town. Damn! I ask if a Lisa Morrison works here. She says "Who?" Guess not.

I get back in my car and head across town. I try his cell phone again. Still off.

I'm gonna beat his ass right there in front of God and everybody. *Messing over me?* Not gonna *have it*! I can see it now. His surprise at seeing me at the site, then WHAM right in the mouth! Got no damn business putting his pecker where it don't belong.

Why is everybody on the damn road this morning? I lean on the horn. Get out of the way*! Is that some more road construction? What does this guy want?!* What? I'm not turning around. How long will the drawbridge be out of order do you think? All day?! I've got to get over to the other side!

I just sit there looking at the bridge, refusing to move, ignoring the blaring from the horns of the cars behind me. He finally tells me to move or he was calling the police. Shit! I turn the car around and head towards home.

Once home, I decided to see if I could find Lisa Morrison in the phone book. B's... E's...K's....M's. Morrison. There's five Lisa Morrison's. Fine. I start at the top. No answer at the first number.

I dial the second. An elderly sounding lady answers. I ask for Lisa Morrison.

"Speaking," she says. Since *surely* she wasn't the one, I told her I was looking for her daughter Lisa. She informs me she has no children and hangs up the phone.

Okay. Third Lisa. A young woman answers. I asked for Lisa Morrison. "Oh, that's me," she replied.

I ask her if she has a child name Shawn.

"Yes, I do. Why?"

Why? Why?

I tell her whose wife I am and that I got a letter saying that she and he have a child. Is this true?

"Yes, he is the father of my child."

I hear a click.

"Hello? Hello?" The bitch hung up on me! That's all right, I call right back. Her answering machine picks up. I call again and again and again. Still the answering machine. I leave a *foul* message.

I'm in a *state* by this time, just *waiting* for his ass to walk in the door. The phone is ringing again. I ignore it, again. It continues ringing until I finally answer it. It's Steve. I tell him to come home now. Something seriously bad has happened. I refuse to tell him what it is over the phone. *If I tell him now, he'll stay out late avoiding me.*

I wait. Clenching and unclenching my hand. Imagining his throat in them.

He arrives home in a flash. Runs through the door.

"What's wrong?!" he shouts in a panic. I pick up the letter and fling it at him. He looks at me like I'm crazy.

"Read it!" I yell at him. He starts reading it, his eyes getting bigger and bigger. His mouth drops open.

I got you now, you bastard. I reach way back to Africa and slap the *hell* out of him. I kick and punch and bite him like he spit on my Moma. I was working up a sweat! *Bring it on Tyson, bring it on!*

He finally pins me to the couch. I can see the imprint from my hand in his face; a lump growing above his eyebrow. His lip has burst, blood dripping down his torn shirt.

"Baby, it ain't me! They got the wrong man!"

"How many men with your name you know?"

"There must be some! I don't know no Lisa Morris, Martin or whatever!"

"Yes you do! I talked to your bitch myself!" I struggle to sit up. I'm gonna punch this lying fucker in the mouth again!

"I'm telling you it ain't *me*! Let me call these folk and find out what the hell is going on! Will you let me do that? *Please*?!"

"Yeah, you call them! Call them now! I'm going to be on the other phone listening in to your every word. Don't even *try* talking in code and shit."

He let me go and backed up fast. Watching me, he retrieved the paper that was now torn and partially wadded up from the floor. He flattened it out and dialed the number. I picked up the kitchen extension and positioned my chair where I could see the motherfucker.

"Social Services, how may I help you?"

"Yes. I received a letter about a paternity test, but there is a mistake. I don't know this woman."

"What is the mother's name?"

64

"Lisa Morrison." He says her name, like he'd said it *plenty* of times before. *Lying asshole*!

"Are you specifically named in the letter?" You damn skippy he is!

"Yes, but I don't know any Lisa Morrison." Lying to the end.

"Are you a white male, aged 26?" *What?*

"No, I'm a black man, aged 40."

"Well, sir, you do not fit the description of the father. As a matter of policy, whenever the alleged father's address is unknown, we send out the letter to all persons in the city with the father's name in an attempt to locate the actual father of a child. When they call in, we verify certain information and if you fit the description, we ask you to voluntarily come in for the paternity test." *Ain't this some shit!* I almost called that woman out of her name right there.

"That's crap, lady! You just about messed up my marriage with some stupid letter!" *Damn right* she did!

"We are sorry for the inconvenience. Just tear up the letter. Thank you for calling. Goodbye."

I hang up the phone and just look at my husband. He just looks at me. I feel foolish as hell. He finally gets up and without a word goes into the bedroom. Closes the door.

Do you think he's mad?

HIGH EDUCATION

I inhale deeply on the blunt and the smoke burns the back of my throat. I cough and smoke snorts through my nose.

"Swallow it!" the girl says.

She must be *tripping*. How the heck am I going to swallow this smoke? I choke and hold in the cough.

"Swallow it! This some good shit. We can't be wasting it!"

I push down the urge to cough and swallow. The smoke burns my esophagus and I feel it settle in my stomach. Burning.

"That's good. Now do it again."

Again?! Is she trying to kill me?

"You ain't gonna feel nothing, unless you do it again."

I draw on the butt, the heat burning my fingertips. I fan the smoke in front of my face.

"Now swallow it."

I swallow. I can feel the tips of my fingers tingling. My lips feel a little numb. Uhm, my arms are relaxing. I pull on the butt again, ignoring the burn in my fingers.

Swallow. Pull. Swallow. I...feel... good! Mellow. Shit!

The butt burns my fingers and I drop it to the ground.

"What'd you do that for?" she asked. She picks the butt off the ground and places it between some miniature clamps—roach clips. "This is still good." She lights it and sucks hard. Cheeks puffed out, holding in the smoke.

I start to giggle. Girl looks like a raccoon—dark circles under her eyes, cheeks puffed out and her hair is standing up in spikes. I take that back. She looks like a scared cat and a raccoon. A Cooncat! This makes me clutch my stomach, howling.

"What the *hell* is so funny?" she asks. I can hardly breathe 'cause I'm laughing so hard. I lean against the car and close my eyes. Maybe if I don't see her, I can stop laughing at her. I feel my heart thumping loudly in my chest. I open my eyes.

What the fu...?

The light from the car stereo is jumping back and forth in front of my face.

Near. Far. Near. Far.

Damn, I shouldn't have closed my eyes! *Take some deep breaths to clear your head!* I suck in a trunkful of air and blow it out fast. The stereo is still jumping.

"Hey. You all right?" She leans towards me, her body jumping near, then far. Near, then far. "Your eyes look kind of wild. You just feeling the rush. It'll be OK in a little while."

67

Her voice sounds like it is coming down through a long tunnel. I have to watch her lips to understand the words coming out of her mouth. *My sister told me not to go out with this girl. Said she was fast and knew way too much for me.* I feel scared and happy and floaty all at the same time.

"Why don't you sit down in the car?" she suggested.

I let her help me into the car, the numbers on the stereo LCD jumping back and forth. Fucking with me. I lean my head back on the headrest and close my eyes.

"I want to go home."

"Home? What the hell for?" she asked.

"I feel funny as hell."

"That's what you are supposed to feel," she replied.

"I don't like this shit here."

"Quit tripping. It's just a little weed. Not no coke or nothing. Anybody can smoke weed."

"I want to go home!" I stated emphatically.

"Now, I know you ain't gonna be no sissypunk are you?" she said.

I opened my eyes. "Sissypunk?!" I yelled. "Who the hell you calling a sissypunk?"

"What?!" The girl looked around wild-eyed.

"Who the hell you calling a sissypunk?" I screamed.

"What are you talking about?" she asked leaning back against the door.

"Oh. You don't remember what you just *said*?!" I snarled.

"Hey, calm down! You tripping. You haven't said a *thing* to me since I got you in the car," she said her fingers splayed in front of her. "Now I don't know who you *thought* you were talking to, but it wasn't me."

"Girl, I'll beat yo' ass. Call me a sissypunk again!" I dared.

The girl opened the car door and took off running into the park.

"Don't nobody call me no sissypunk!" I hollered through the window. I watch her sit on a bench facing towards the car.

Trifling heifer, calling me damn names. I'll kick her ass. Where are the damn car keys? Shit! She got the keys. I sit there in the car with the windows down. The cold air dampening my buzz. I lean back into the seat and close my eyes.

"You lost?"

Huh? Who is that? I open my eyes and find myself looking at this phat chick! It's this girl from school. What's her name? Foxy L or something.

"Ain't nobody else here. You lost?" Foxy L says.

I look around and don't see my girl. "I guess this girl I was with left me."

69

"I'll give you a ride home. I've seen you at school. You the running back on the football team," she says.

"Yeah, I play a little football."

Now I remember. She's a "season girl." She screws athletes depending on what season it is. Football season, football players. Basketball season, basketball players. Hot damn, it's football season now!

"I really get off watching all y'all dressed up in your suits with those tights pants on." Her voice sounds different that a few moments ago. Deeper. Maybe she is hoarse. I just ignore it.

I get into her car. Warm. I rub my arms to get the circulation going.

"Now you don't really want to go home right away, do you?" Foxy asks.

"Naw, I can stay out a while and talk and stuff. Whatever you want to do."

"Look, let's cut to the chase. I want to jump your bones. Now. Right here." Foxy says.

Mercy, mercy me. I must be living right.

"Baby, I'm game, if you game." I ain't gonna pass up this opportunity!

We get into the back seat and start kissing. Really tonguing it. Oh, the passion in her kisses! She gonna have a monster under there boy! I lift her skirt and feel up her legs. She is moaning. "Yes. Yes." I pull her panties down and go for the gold.

OH SHIT! What the hell am I feeling?! I pull up the skirt and just about faint.

She has a prick!

It's bigger than mine!

"Now I know you ain't surprised. Everybody knows I'm a boy" she/he said, sounding like George Jefferson. "What you like? Tops? Bottoms? I can work it either way," she/he said stroking her/himself.

I back up and find the car door, release the handle and fall backwards onto the ground.

"How you feeling now?" my girl asked me.

Huh? What the hell is going on? "What?"

"You were sleeping then you started moving about like you was having fits and just about fell out the car. I figured you had probably calmed down enough to act reasonable," she said rolling her eyes.

"I was sleep?" *Please let it have been a dream.*

"Yeah. Just for a few minutes. I tried to wait as long as I could, but damn, it's cold out there. I don't know *what* you *think* I said but I'm going to apologize anyway."

"Has anybody else been here?"

"Like who? Ain't nobody else fool enough to be out here. *Who* you looking *for?*" she said popping her head.

71

I look up at the sky and clasp my hands together. Thankyouthankyouthankyouthankyouthankyouthankyou *ThankYou*!

"Junior, what's wrong with you?"

"Nothing. I think we should be getting home," I said, grateful down to the soles of my feet.

"All right then. You sure you feeling OK. You still acting strange."

"I'm fine. Really, fine." She stared at me for a minute then she backed the car out onto the road and drove me home.

I reflect over the night and I'm *still* trembling. What if that hadn't been a dream! I'll never look at Foxy L the same. Is she really a boy? I wonder if anybody else has tripped this bad before. Then, why are they still smoking it? Ain't no telling what I would have imagined or even done if I had smoked crack or meth or something. I shake my head. I just want to get home. Wash my mouth out! I swear, I'll NEVER, as long as I live, smoke weed again. It'll get you messed up *bad*. Leave that shit alone!

DIG-DUG-DUGGED

Hello ladies. I know y'all are wondering what the hell damn business I've got even *talking* to you. Listen up, any damn way. Now y'all call me a "golddigger," and a home wrecker, just because I know what I want and go after it. I prefer the title "Connoisseur of Financially Fit Men." Sounds so much better than "golddigger," doesn't it? I love and leave 'em and I always come out on top.

I used to be just like you. Giving my all for love. Living from paycheck to hope-the-paycheck-comes-before-the-light-man-does. Every dollar I made, *already* had somebody else's name penciled in beside George's head.

Raggedy ass, roach motel apartments. A car with the fuel hand always on "E"nough. Walmarts was like a Dillards to me then. All this *and* I had a man I loooved. Shit, I was living the Great Russian Dream or something!

Well girl, do you know, while *I* was giving my *all* to the man I loooved, he was giving *his all* to some ugly Judyflip across town. I'm being nice when I say ugly—an ass big enough to set a table of six down to dinner; you could serve dessert on her belly; and hair that wasn't long as dust on a jug. If she didn't have size 14 feet, I'll kiss a monkey's ass. Oh and that *face!* Let's just say, y'all have all heard the joke about the Gorilla cookies, right?

I changed my stupid ways right then and there. I don't "love" for free. A broke brother can't do *nothing* for this sister. If he is broke when you get him, he'll be broke when you are done with him. And YOU will be broker than when you started.

Between jobs? Keep stepping.

Don't say my name, if you ain't got change.

Y'all saying that love is better than money. Then explain some of this to me. Why is it that the same man that *loves* you can't bring his paycheck home? If he *loved* you he would make sure you had what you needed, right?

Why is it that the same man that *loves* you, can't keep a job? He knows he has responsibilities, so why can't he get along with the folks at work so the bills can get paid?

Why is it that the same man that *loves* you will buy a car requiring more than half of his paycheck for the car payment, then bum gas money off you the rest of the month? Can he count?

Why is it that the same man that *loves* you will let you work two or three jobs to pay the bills and he won't even have dinner waiting when you get home?! Don't you get hungry?

Why is it that the same man that *loves* you will "borrow" your last two dollars for bus fare to buy a forty? Ain't it 25 degrees out there today?

Puh-leese!

Love works for some people, just not me. Been there, done that and got my ass spanked good.

I need cold, hard cash. Benjamins preferably. See, money comes home when I do. Money gets me food when I want it, gas when I need it, and pays bills when they are due. Money don't get tired. Money don't get disrespectful. Money don't say can't. Money is a great equalizer. Money makes this big old crazy world go 'round and 'round.

I'm not right, you say? Oh, I'm more than right. Men will suck the life and money right out of you. See, men think about us a lot differently than we think about them. We pamper them, stand behind them in whatever, massage their egos even when they ain't about shit, and do for them when we *need* to be doing for *ourselves*. We'll give a no-good man our *last* dollar.

Men, on the other hand, tell you plenty of sweet stuff while the hunt is on, but when they get you…that sweet stuff don't come out again unless you write your biography. Men do for us after they have done for themselves. They ask us to accept things they won't accept. They want a lady in the street, a whore in the bedroom *and* you need to take your ass to work. Think you'll get their last dollar? You'll just be waiting.

Commitment you say? What good is commitment when he won't do right? Girl, love will get you *committed*. Fast. The only commitment I need from my money is that it ain't counterfeit. My money is committed to me until it leaves my hands. After that, I ain't looking for that piece of change any more.

Yeah, you got his ring on your finger but, believe it or not, they'll sell *you* rings for your fingers too. You can take them off whenever you damn well please.

I deserve the good things out of life. I ain't working for free. Got cash? You might get some ass. Shit, I like being wined and dined. I like getting "gifts" and going on trips. I like shopping at Dillards and Saks and them other scared-to-go-in-when-you-are-broke stores.

When was the last time you had a vacation you didn't pay for? When was the last time your man took you out and wined and dined you at some place that didn't have a buffet or a drive thru window?

Get real!

Ladies, you got to work out and work up! Get yourself in "fighting" shape and work up to the type of man you really deserve. Accentuate the positives and downplay them negatives. Bad hair? Get you some good weave. "Long distance" teeth? Get dentures. No boobs?

Get a Wonderbra until you can afford surgery. Become all the woman you always hoped to be.

Now when I start "digging" at a brother, he gone get dug straight the hell out! I *gots* the sexy shit from Frederick's. My hair gets done once or twice a week. I don't *miss* a nail appointment. I am always *fresh*. This dog bought her some books and videos and learned some new tricks, too. I praise him and haze him at the same time. I don't have no problem getting "gifts."

Don't hate. Relate. It's bad men that made me the wonderful woman I am today. Like that old song says:

Your loving gives me such a thrill
But love don't pay my bills
I need Moooooney
That's what I want!

Join me?

ON THE DOLE

"Shequana! Quanisha! Mufar! Jamal! Latonia! The bus is coming down the road! Y'all ain't even ready!"

Dag. We overslept again! That ain't nothing new. If them kids get to school three days a week I'm doing good. I get sick and tired of that school calling me asking why they ain't in school. Why they think? They ain't in school cause they at home. Are them teachers dumb or what! It's a wonder these kids learn anything down there.

"Y'all go in there and watch some TV and let Mama get some more sleep." I yawn and lay back down. My head is killing me. I know they got some cereal to eat. I don't think I got anymore milk, though. Well, cereal and water is better than nothing at all. I'll get some groceries later on today.

We had a good time at the High Rollers Club last night! Me and my girl, Gigi, wore them fellas out! I was decked down in my Tommy jeans and shirt. I got my hair and nails done yesterday. I was the bomb!

There was an old pimp in the club. I wish you could have seen him—leisure suit, Kango hat and shades. He was showing the money though! Gigi was all over him like a stain. He bought us drink after drink and that's why my head is hurting so bad this morning. He got on the dance floor once or twice, but only on the slow numbers. Gigi gave him her cell phone number before we left. I don't know why? Ain't no man gonna stay around Gigi long with them four bad ass kids of hers.

"Cut that TV down!" I hollered. The noise is about to drive me out of my mind! Why did them kids pick this day to oversleep?

"Mama, can we go outside?" Jamal asked.

"No, you cannot." I sniffed the air. Something or *somebody* smelled like day-old pee. "When was the last time you took a bath, Jamal?"

"Uh, I took one day before yesterday."

"Get your stinky butt in that tub! Now!"

All these kids. I love them to death. I hope they know it 'cause their Daddies ain't worth a flip.

I had Shequana and Quanisha with my high school sweetheart. We was suppose to get married when we finished high school. But just as soon as he finished, he told me he didn't want to marry me. He was going to school to have a better life. Where the hell is this better life? I want it too. He know damn well he was born in the projects and will die in the projects. Shoot, my Moma lived here all her life and all my sisters do too. Don't *nobody* get out.

He said he didn't have no money when he went off to college. He gave me $100 every now and then when his financial aid came through. It wasn't enough to keep my babies in diapers. Eventually, he stopped coming round whenever he was home and stopped bringing me any money for these girls. When I found out he had gotten married, I whacked out! Ain't got no money for our girls, but he can get his butt *married*?

I got me some legal advice and filed support on him. Now, I get $700 a month for the both of them. He had the nerve to call and tell me he could hardly live with all the money they was taking out of his check! So? These girls got needs too. I didn't get them by myself.

He told the judge that I lived in public housing and I only paid $15 a month in rent. Said I was getting food stamps and Medicaid for my kids. What did I need all that money for? I told that judge that my girls deserved better than I had. That $700 was necessary for them to get what they needed. He then told the judge he was married and had his own responsibilities. The judge reminded him that these girls were his responsibility too. Booya!

Mufar's daddy wasn't no better. He was married when we started messing around. He said he didn't want to use no "skins" because he didn't like how it felt. He wanted to "feel" me. Well, he knew I wasn't on the pill and didn't have no implants or IUD, so why he wanna trip when I get pregnant? Had the nerve to say I tried to trap him! How did I trap him? He was already married. Besides, he was the one running *me* down.

I had to cuss out that high yellow wife of his. She come calling me talking about I tried to hoodwink him by getting a baby with him and they wasn't going to pay me *shit*! Said she was gonna have me locked up for using their credit card illegally. How did I use it illegally and he gave me one of my own? My name's on it, not her's.

I showed her ass. I filed papers just as soon as Mufar was born. Got his ass dragged in for a blood test that proved he was the father.

I know who my babies' daddies are! I ain't no hood rat.

She was royally pissed off when I named Mufar after his daddy. Well that $400 a month should shut her up!

Then here his daddy come apologizing for his wife. You know he *begged* me for some coochie. I suggested he take his ass home before his wife found out about him being over here. I'd hate to have to split her head open, but I will. He still sneaking his ass over here visiting Mufar and begging for some.

Now, I thought Jamal's daddy was going to be my knight in shining armor. He was so *good* to me. Gave me money every and I mean ev-e-ry week. Paid my utilities, got me a phone and bought us a used car. He seemed to like my kids too. Always taking the girls to the park and movies and stuff. He fixed their breakfast and lunches and picked them up after school. I know sometimes the girls said they didn't want to go with him, but he was good with them, kept them out of my hair.

Like they say though, if it seems too good to be true it usually is. One day, I left home going to the mall when I realized that I had forgotten the money I needed to get out a layaway. I turned right around and headed home to get it. I heard him in the bathroom with the girls when I walked in the door. Something just didn't *feel* right though. I crept down the hall to find out what was going on. He didn't hear me over the bathwater running. I walked in on that dirty dog with his mouth on my Quanisha's chest. Both of them girls was naked! I guess he wasn't expecting me.

I hollered like a banshee and commenced to tear that motherfucker a new asshole! Broke *every one* of my goddamn nails off in his face. Messing with children! What kind of shit is that? I put his ass out! Threw his damn clothes out on the sidewalk! That fucker left and took the car with him. My girls are still in therapy.

I found out I was pregnant two weeks after that shit had happened. *I don't believe in abortions!* Besides, Jamal is a "love child." His daddy is just fucked up in the head.

82

You know I filed papers on his ass. They send me a whopping $250 a month. He had the nerve to bring his ass over here saying he wanted to spend time with his son since he had to pay for him. I went straight down to the courthouse and got me a restraining order. *This woman ain't gonna let no pervert be around her kids!*

Latonia's daddy was a mistake from day one. He was a small time drug dealer, but girl, he was pretty drink of water. I'm telling you, he wasn't no good *at all.*
I don't know *what* came over me. Shit, he already had eight kids by six other women, but I just didn't care. I wanted that man and I got him. He was stingy with the money and came to see me maybe once a week at the most. But when he came, I treated him like a king! Got Gigi to watch my kids and we had us a *gooooood* time.

Unfortunately, the life expectancy of a drug dealer is short. He was shot down in the street when Latonia was 2 months old. I felt like dying myself. I miss that man to this day!

I filed for Social Security after he died. They sending me $418 a month for her until she turn 18. I notice that she acts kind of "slow," so I might need to file for a "crazy check" too. Gigi get them checks for two of her kids. That would be another $3-400 right there. I need to call down there and find out what we need to do 'cause I could use the extra money. Them kids want a Dreamcast and a computer for Christmas.

I put on a FUBU sweatsuit and head for the grocery store. I leave the kids at home since I need some time to myself. I walk four blocks and enter a parking garage. Going up two flights of stairs, I get into my SUV. I know I ain't supposed to have anything worth more than $3,000, but what they don't know won't hurt. Besides, with all them kids, I need something to get around in.

I put it in my Moma's name. She died two years ago, but they haven't figured that out yet. I just keep up the payments and the insurance. The kids think I borrow it from one of my friends to run errands. That's all they need to think. It's all good.

I tool over to the W&P and fill up two shopping carts. When I check out, I pull out my food stamp card for the cashier to scan. I hear the woman behind me telling somebody else that it's a shame that her father and mother worked 40 years and they can't get but $15 in food stamp credit. She bets that I got a house full of snot-nosed kids. I ignore her and ask that they deliver my groceries to the apartment.

Makes me sick the way people always assuming shit. I'm a stay at home mother. My kids need this food. Don't be mad at me because you have to work!

84

I go to the mall to get my kids some clothes. Banana Republic, Osh Kosh, FUBU. My kids wear only the best. Let me pick up some sneakers. Oh good, the new Jordan's are out. They are on sale for $179.00. I get a pair for each of the boys. Is that a leather jacket sale? I get a maxicoat for myself. I've got something for everybody. Time to go.

I retrace my route and park the SUV back in the parking garage. I hail a cab and take the packages home. The kids are still watching TV and playing Nintendo. All is well. I give the kids their stuff and go to the bedroom and lie down. My head is still killing me. I sigh and cut out the light.

Home sweet home. On you!

THE SHOW

I pause in the foyer and look over the people gathered in the sanctuary for today's service. It's a full crowd this morning. I rub my hands, eager to get down to business. Here comes Deacon Myers with my robe. Good. Let's get started.

I step onto the raised platform and a hush falls over the crowd. I look at the piano player and she begins to play. I start out with a low moan to work up the spirit a little bit. The ladies start to moan with me. I lead into my prayer with a low, mournful tone, the quiet punctuated by outbursts from the crowd. *Yes. Be with me. Oh I want to thank you! You've been so good to me.*

My praying gets loud and fast. I open my eyes to gauge the crowd. I can tell by the uplifted arms and the swaying in the seats, they are feeling it. The organ begins with a fast beat. The voices crescendo and blend together. I segue into a song. My voice is off-key and broken, but the crowd sings with me and nobody notices.

Ms. Lila jumps up and down with the spirit. Somebody catch her! Last week she squashed a whole row of children when she fell back *and* she cracked the bench. She cutting into my money. I had to pay them children's doctor bills! Why do the women who get the spirit always weigh 300+ pounds?

I holler. The organ blasts some shouting chords. I holler again. The organ blasts some more chords. Here we go! I'm working it now! Ms. Lila starts flapping her arms around and accidentally slaps a lady holding her baby. The ushers run up the aisle and try to grab her arms. She's flapping her arms so hard, she knocks the handkerchief off one of the ushers' head. She is slap out of control!

Let me tone this thing down before I have to pay some more doctor bills!

I glance at the piano player and the organist and hold up one finger. Immediately, the music softens. The ushers have managed to get a hold of Ms. Lila's hands and sit her back down. They fan her, their butts in the faces of the people in the next row. It's quieting. I still got it after all these years…

I opened this worship hall nearly ten years ago, after the last place I preached gave me a little trouble. They had a board of Trustees I had to report to, regulations about the topics of my sermons, no house to live in, an old car for my family to use and they didn't pay me worth a flip. They were just a no class set of hypocrites.

I wasn't meant to be no poor mouth pastor. I was shooting for plenty of bounty in my life. I worked my *tail off* for those people! After the first revival I held for them, they collected nearly $10,000. Do you know how much of that money I got? My regular salary plus $500. I asked about the Love offering they took up for me. The report said it was $2,500. They told me that they didn't give more than $500 to any preacher for the Love Offering. I could take the $500 or take nothing. After I rebelled and gave a sermon on "The Joys of Sex," they asked me to leave. I took half of the congregation with me and started this ministry. No Trustees to report to and I keep the bankbook.

My folks are good to me! They like good things and they want me to have good things too. Just last month, they gave me a Mercedes for Pastor Appreciation Day. Now that's the kind of appreciation I like. They told me they wanted me to look prosperous, so, I bought a seven-bedroom mansion on three acres just outside of town. It has a swimming pool, a Jacuzzi *and* a tennis court.

I did have to give a sermon entitled "A Little In Equals A Little Out" on tithing when the collection was down one month. I thought I was going to have to cancel my Missionary Outreach trip to the resort in Aruba.

Now, don't misjudge me. There are plenty of lost souls out there "creeping" at these resorts and it is my mission to try to change their ways. I have been able to really *touch* folks on my missionary trips to Honolulu,

Cancun` and Paris. It's a shame I am working so hard on these trips that my wife can't join me. Anyway, she would be *mortified* if she saw women walking around bare-chested, wearing only dental floss, laying out in the sun like they do at some of those places. Shameful! I must have a clear mind when I'm in the Devil's den, trying to reach out to these poor souls. Sometimes I have to use any means necessary to reach them. I can't do that if I'm worried about the little wife's state of mind, now can I? Well...

I start my sermon "Being Broke is Hell on Earth." The audience sits rapt, attentive to my every word. After all, I know what I am talking about.

Halfway through the sermon, Mrs. Jesse's daughter gets up to take a child to the bathroom. *Goodness me, that girl sure fills out her skirt!* I try not to glance at her behind as she walks in front of my podium. I'm going to have to talk to Mrs. Jesse about baptizing her. I can see her in that sheet right now waiting for me to dunk her under the water. After the dunking, the sheet clings everywhere, leaving nothing to the imagination.... Let me finish this sermon and talk to her. I don't want that girl to get into no evil before I get to her!

I close out the sermon, imploring those who want to be saved to come forward. The lady with the baby comes along with two children. Mrs. Jesse's daughter *doesn't* come up. I see now I'm going to have to work on those folk.

I glance over at Deacon Myers and he is pulling at his collar, sweat running down his face. *What is wrong with him?* The secretary is telling the crowd that the lady and her children are candidates for baptism. There is loud clapping throughout the church. Deacon Myers has a coughing fit.

Somebody give that man some water!

The lady wants to say a few words. I relax back in my chair, eager for her to get over with her statement. She begins telling us that she is a sinner and wants to change her ways. She has never been married and her children are all "love" children and she needs to repent. She then tells us that she chose this church because the children's daddy is a member here.

I sit up in my seat.

She then names the children's father…Deacon Myers.

Good goobley goo!

Pandemonium explodes throughout the building. I look over at Deacon Myers and he clutches his chest and slumps into the pew. Three ushers were trying to restrain Mrs. Myers. She got loose anyhow, hauled off and kicked Deacon Myers in the groin! *Thank goodness he had already passed out!* The other deacons dragged Deacon Myers from the room.

My wife hops into the woman's face and demands that she retract that outrageous lie! Deacon Myers is a pillar of the community! The woman told my wife that Deacon Myers has been "dating" her since she was sixteen. He had bought her a house near the beach and a Lexus. All the kids were his. He was there for every one of their births and he was listed as the father on the birth certificates. Anyway, Mrs. Myers already knew about her. She had been calling her disgusting names on the telephone all week.

My wife sat down hard!

I cleared my throat and asked that everyone be seated. They ignored my first request. I asked again that everyone remain calm and just take a seat. Finally, everyone sat down. Somebody was crying loudly in the back. The ushers were holding Mrs. Myers tight.

I told them that Deacon Myers was only a man and as a man makes mistakes. Let us all keep him in out hearts and minds and be not quick to judge him.

A deacon whispered that we should just skip the collection and dismiss. No way. I need the money for the ministry! I gave the signal to the choir director for a song. The spirit had left the building though. I could see that the collection plates were not nearly as full as usual. *Messing with my money again!*

I dismissed from the podium. The people stampeded the doors getting out of there! *My telephone is going to be jumping tonight.*

My wife sat on the front pew still in shock. I went to her and put my arms around her. She *slapped* me! Right there! I couldn't believe it. She said that as close as I was to Deacon Myers, I probably already knew about this mess! *Yes, I knew he had a "fly" problem, but all I can do is advise. I can't make him stop.* She then accused *me* of improper behavior with some women in the congregation! Told me that she overheard some women talking about some special "healing" sessions I was giving to young women. I was stunned. *I'm firing every one of these big mouth fools I got around me.* She jumped up and said she had a mind to ask one of those women about those "healing" sessions right now! I tried to stop her, but she hit me in the face with one of the metal water goblets on the podium.

My wife stormed out of the front doors. My heart dropped as I see her go. I heard loud voices, then arguing. *Are they cursing?* I struggled to my feet and run into the parking lot. My wife had a woman in a chokehold up against a car, cussing for all she was worth. The woman was struggling and the people were crowded around just looking. She shoved that girl to the ground before I reached them. I wanted to help the woman up, but I thought it would look bad, so I just talked to her and looked too.

I hear a car crank up and I turn in time to see my Mercedes swerve to miss some people. Rocks fly as my wife peels out of the parking lot. The woman hops in her car and leaves. The people begin to disperse. They don't talk to me at all like they usually do.

I told Myers time and time again, you can't keep doing this shit! Half them folks are never going to come here again. I sigh. I guess I will have to let him go.

I walk slowly back into the building. The young woman who was crying is still sitting on the last pew so I walk up to her and ask what is wrong. She says she needs "healing." Bad. Right now. I sigh again and ask her to come to my office. As she walks by, I can see by the way her hips shake, she don't know what a girdle is.

I look up at the ceiling, hoping for some kind of sign. Any kind of sign.

The Bible falls off the podium. *There it is!*

I walk to my office and close the door. I got some "ministering" to do. After all, they don't give me all of their money for nothing. The show *must* go on.

DUMB AND DUMBER

I sigh as I look at the case placed in front of me. The courtroom has a circus atmosphere—people milling about, babies crying and general background noise of talking and laughing. Just another jammed packed day in Small Claims Court.

Let's see...hmmm, this one ought to be interesting. The plaintiff claims that the defendant has unknowingly used her charge cards and bought more than $3,000 in merchandise. The defendant's defense is that she is on the account and has the right to buy the goods. Well, let's get on with it and see what's what. I nod at Mingo, the bailiff.

"All rise! Small Claims Court of the Second Circuit come to order. The Honorable Marcus Tilton, residing," Mingo's deep baritone booms out.

The talking ceases and rustling is heard as people take their seats. Babies are shushed or taken outside the doors. I settle myself in the tall black leather chair and arrange my hot robe around me. As I lean back, I kick off my shoes and scratch at my ankles with my big toe.

"The next case on the docket is Hammond versus Johnson. All parties involved please come forward," Mingo booms out.

I watch as two women—one, a "high yellow" with black hair tied up in a too little pony-tail and wearing sweat pants; and the other, darker with platinum blond hair, skin-tight pants and a passel of kids with her— navigate past the other people on their row and try the ignore each other as they take their respective places in front of my bench. I glance back at the file to obtain the correct names before continuing.

"Mrs. Hammond, is it?" I look at the plaintiff and she nods her head, "What seems to be the problem?"

"Well Your Honor, this *woman* stole my credit card and charged up quite a large bill."

"Do you have proof?"

"I sure do." Mrs. Hammond flips through a manila folder she has brought with her, removes three pieces of paper and hands them to Mingo.

Scanning it, I notice numerous charges over a three-month period, totaling $2,987.00.

"Okay. Ms. Johnson, what do you know about this?" I turn to the defendant and ask.

Ms. Johnson scratches at her scalp and runs her tongue over her lips before she answers. "Ah…I was told I could buy the stuff. I haven't stolen anything from this woman and she knows it," she finishes by rolling her eyes at the plaintiff.

"That woman is lying!" BAM! BAM! BAM! "I haven't told her she could buy a *durn thing* with my card. I don't even *know* her that well!"

"Mrs. Hammond, this is *my* courtroom. You don't speak unless I tell you to. I don't plan to remind you again," I say in my sternest tone.

"Yes, Your Honor."

"Now, Ms. Johnson, you say that you were told you could charge this merchandise to her card."

"That's right," she nods affirmative, her gum popping loudly as she speaks.

"By whom?"

"Well...Your Honor, I just want to say...she already knows by who and we are just wasting everybody's time by being here."

"That's for me to judge. If you indeed are buying things using a stolen credit card, that is a very serious offense punishable by jail time." I smile inwardly as her eyes grow round as apples. "Again, who told you that you could charge the merchandise to this card account?"

"Her husband." The crowd erupts in hoots, loud laughter and whistles.

"That a damn lie!" BAM! BAM! BAM! "My husband hadn't...," BAM! "...told nobody they could charge *shit*...," BAM! "... on my card!" BAM! BAM!

BAM! Mrs. Hammond manages to finish even though I'm banging the gavel like hell.

"Mrs. Hammond! One more outburst and your case will be dismissed."

"But…"

"Ah! Not another word, unless I request that you speak. Do you understand me? Another word and you and your case can walk out the door."

"Yessir," she says reluctantly, staring knives into the defendant who, petulantly, stares back.

"Now. Ms. Johnson, you say that the plaintiff's *husband* told you that you could use Mrs. Hammond's card to buy things?"

"I didn't use *her* card, but that's correct."

"All right. Now, Mrs. Hammond, you didn't know anything about these charges?"

"No! There is *no way* that my husband would tell anybody they could use our credit card."

"Our? Is he on the account also?"

"Yes, he is."

"How do you know that Ms. Johnson and not Mr. Hammond made these charges? How did you guess it was her in the first place?"

"Your Honor, I didn't guess, I *know* it was her. When I got the first bill, it wasn't too high…if you look on that first month's bill, you'll see it near the bottom…well, I asked him about the charges and...ah, I forget now what he said it was about. Anyway, I didn't think too much about it. But, when I received the second one, I called the card company and requested a copy of the receipts. Before I got the copies, I got the third bill...look on that last sheet...yes, that's it...I almost had a stroke when I saw how much it was. I was on the phone immediately, trying to figure out what was going on."

"So, when you got the copies what did you find out?"

"I got a bunch of receipts with her name scribbled all over the bottom of them. I asked my husband if he knew who Jaquinta Johnson was and he said he didn't know anybody by that name."

"He's lying. He knows...," BAM! BAM! "...me and she does too!" BAM!

I take off my glasses, rub my nose and stare at the two women. Enunciating slowly, I say, "Do you both understand English? Didn't I say not to speak unless I asked you to? What, exactly, are you all confused about here?"

"Your Honor, that heifer is lying! I can hardly stand here while she lies about everything!" Mrs. Hammond says huffily, her body trembling in fury.

"Yes you can and you will. Otherwise, I will hold you in contempt and dismiss your case. Understand?" I look at both of them.

"Yes."

"Yessir."

"Now, your husband says he doesn't know anything about these charges, is that correct?"

"Yes."

"Do you think he might be lying to you?"

"No! He doesn't have any reason to be lying. He said he didn't charge these things and I believe him!"

"Okay then. Ms. Johnson, what proof do you have that you could legally use this card?"

Ms. Johnson, apparently waiting for this moment, pulls open her purse, extracts an envelope and removes a credit card.

"See? My names on this card and it's the one I used," she holds out the card triumphantly.

Mingo retrieves the card, looks at it and can't help but smirk as he hands it to me. Comparing the numbers, I see that they matched with the account.

"Mrs. Hammond, this card with Ms. Johnson's name on it, has the same number that is on the account."

"It can't be, Your Honor. I barely know this woman and I didn't authorize giving her no card!"

"Well, this card number definitely matches the one on the bill. So, do you think the card company made a mistake?"

"Well...."

"Did you inquire about that?"

"Yes, I did."

"What did they tell you?" I lean back in my chair. I already know the deal and I guess chick here just wants to be in denial a little longer.

"They said…they said…I'm so confused here, I'm not really sure what they said."

I nod my head and turn to the defendant. "Ms. Johnson, how did you get this card?"

"Her husband gave it to me."

I see Mrs. Hammond about to make an outburst and I hold up my finger. "*Why* did he give it to you? Mrs. Hammond says she doesn't really know you and all…just *why* would Mr. Hammond give you a card?"

Her face takes on a smug look, "I don't know. I guess he thought I needed some things. Some necessities."

"You needed some things. Necessities." I scan through the receipts to examine the list of items purchased. "You charged some groceries…a pair of Jordan sneakers…a leather coat…some personal items… and a $2,000 diamond ring. I guess this ring was a necessity?"

"That was a present."

"A present. To yourself?"

"No. From Mr. Hammond."

"Mr. Hammond. He told you to go out and buy a $2,000 ring and just charge it as a present."

"Yes."

I shake my head at the stupidity of it all. It's obvious that this man knows this other woman a *lot* better than he is telling his wife.

"Why? Was it a special occasion or something?"

"You might say that."

"Like?" I wave my hands for her to elaborate.

"Well, it was to celebrate the birth of our son."

The courtroom explodes. I bang the gavel right and left, until I finally break it. Mrs. Hammond has crossed over to the defendant and is right in her face, spittle flying as she speaks a hundred miles a minute. Mingo gets between them, holding them arms-length apart as they trade curses and attempt to flail at each other.

"Bitch! You telling a damn lie! I'm gonna…,"

"I ain't lying. You already know the deal. Why the fuck we up in here, I don't know and…"

"…beat the hair off your welfare 'ho ass. You been trying to…"

"…you know he gave me the card! You trying to act like it's all me and shit, but you and I both know that…"

"…fuck with us and I'm *sick* of it. I'm gonna kill your skinny ass today, if it's the *last thing* I…"

"…he did. So, you can…"

I reach under my desk, retrieve my shoe and begin banging it loudly on the desk. It takes a few minutes, but finally everyone returns to their seats and Mingo leads Mrs. Hammond back over to the plaintiff's podium.

"Now, *look* people! This is the last, and I do mean the *last* time, I will repeat myself. If anyone, and that includes every person here, makes another outburst in this courtroom, I will clear it. I don't want to hear any body else speaking unless I ask them to. Got it?!"

I turn my attention back to the defendant. "Ms. Johnson, now you say Mr. Hammond told you to buy this $2,000 ring to celebrate the birth of your son?"

"That's correct."

"Mrs. Hammond, did you know about this child?"

"I didn't know nothing about no child. She's just lying."

"Ms. Johnson?" I turn to her, since she is waving her arms like an air traffic controller to gain my attention.

"She's lying. Here is a copy of the paternity test. Read what it says on the bottom. And here's a copy of the child support papers. I'm getting $400 a month."

Taking a moment to read through the papers given to Mingo, I see that indeed, a Mufar Hammond has been found to 99.9% certain to be the father of her son and that enforced child support is in place.

Looking at Mrs. Hammond, who is now looking at the floor, I say, "Have you seen this?"

"Maybe."

"Take it over there and let her have a look at it Mingo." I hand him the paper. Mrs. Hammond barely glances at it when he places it before her.

"Now, that paper says that he is most likely the father of her child, in fact, it says that y'all are paying child support for this child. So, it seems to me that it's *possible* that Mr. Hammond may have given her an additional card on you all's account after all."

"Your Honor, I asked him and he says he doesn't know anything about this $2,000 charge. He didn't authorize any charge."

"Mrs. Hammond, why is it so hard...*where* is Mr. Hammond today? This is his mess and he should be here. Where is he?" I scan the courtroom, not really expecting to see him.

"He's not here."

"Not here. Where is he? Didn't he know you were coming to court and why? I would think that he would want to be here to clear his name and all."

"He's out of town."

"On business? What does he do?"

"He's unemployed right now. He...he and some of his buddies are on a fishing trip."

I am outraged by the stupidity of this woman. "This woman, who this paper indicates had *his* son, has made a *huge* charge on *y'all's* credit card and he goes on a fishing trip the day you go to court? Not looking for a job, but on a fishing trip? Now don't you think that's just a little *strange*, Mrs. Hammond?" I roll my eyes.

"No. They had been planning this trip for a long time and..."

"Mrs. Hammond, who is paying this child support if he is unemployed?"

Still looking at the floor, she says, "I am."

I pinch the bridge of my nose as I collect my thoughts. "Mrs. Hammond, this is what I see. One, your husband knows this woman *way* better than he has told you. In fact, they were involved at some point. These papers *right... here* tell that story!" I wave the papers, exasperated.

"Two, your husband, unknowing *to you*, filled out the form and got an additional card for Ms. Johnson, which he can do since this is apparently a joint account. Three, Ms. Johnson, whether with his approval or not, charged an expensive ring which was legally within her rights to do so."

Mrs. Hammond looks ready to explode by this time, but I continue anyway. "Mrs. Hammond, Ms. Johnson is acting within the rights, that *your husband* apparently gave her, and legally can buy anything she wants. Now, if you think she forged his name and all, that's another case. I don't see any evidence indicating that presented here. Do you have any?" She shakes her head in the negative.

"Well, then, since Mr. Hammond is absent today, I have no choice but to dismiss this case on no merit."

The defendant stretches her hands towards heaven and yells out, *"Thank ya! Aboloboyama! Thank Ya! The truth has set me free! Thank Ya!"* I *know* she didn't go there!

"One last thing, though," I say as the defendant continues to mumble incoherently and hugs herself. "If I were both of you, I would go fishing and throw this minnow back and try to catch a bass. Good day!"

I rise quickly and exit out the side door. Entering my chambers, I shake my head. How many women gonna continue eating this bullshit before the worms finally eat some sense into their brains?

Mingo pops his head inside the door. "Ready for Round Two?" he says with a wide grin.

"You bet. I wouldn't miss this for the world. Men 1; women 0. Let's see how the rest of the night works out."

Pulling out his wallet and extracting a ten dollar bill, Mingo says, "I've got a tenner that says the men will rule the day."

"I've got a ten that says the women are gonna come back strong," I say, reaching for my wallet.

"I hate to keep taking your money, but I've told you time and time again, a man's motto is 'If you see a fool, keep bumping her head.' We ain't seeing nothing but pure dumbness from these women. I would have picked up on some of that stuff a long time ago and put my foot up my woman's ass."

"Mingo, you a fool."

"No, judge, *they* are."

Laughing, we close the door and stroll into the hallway.

Let the games begin!

PARENT'S RULES

Whap! Whap!

I cover my head so that the belt doesn't hit my face.

Whap!

My butt is *stinging*! I'm not gonna cry…I'm not gonna cry…I'm not gonna cry…

Whap!

The tears stream down my face.

Whap!

I can't take it anymore.

"Wait! Moma *wait*!" I yell. She ignores me and slings the belt again. I catch it in mid-air. She pulls and pushes trying to get the belt out of my hands.

"Wait! Moma *please*!" I holler. The belt slips out of my hands. Oh shit! I take off running with Moma in hot pursuit.

"Don't you run from me girl!" she yells. I run around the table. First one way and then the other, trying to stay out of her reach. She slings the belt across the table.

Whap! The new flower vase falls off the table and breaks.

"See what you made me do?" she screams. "I'm gonna beat your ass if it's the last thing I do!"

I break for the door. *If I can just make it out of the door, I'm gonna run until I pass out.* Moma grabs my shirt and stops me short.

Whap! Whap! Whap! I'm writhing on the floor, screaming.

"I told you time and time again, I'm the Moma! You the child!"

Whap!

"Do you understand me?!"

Whap!

"Yes! I under.. hic…stand you!"

"When I say come home, YOU come home!" *Whap!*

"Yes, Moma!" *She is killing me!*

"That don't mean when YOU feel like it, it means when I say. Understand?!"

Whap!

"Yes, Moma!"

"If you grown, then get out of my house and pay for your own shit!"

"I ain't grown, Moma. I ain't grown!"

"Now get out of my sight until I ask to see you again. And shut up all that noise before I give you something to cry about."

I get up off the floor slowly, mumbling under my breath, "I hate that old witch. She makes me sick!"

"What did you say, girl?" Moma turns and asks. "You say you need me to put this strap on your behind some more?"

"No, Moma! I didn't say nothing!" I cried out.

"That's what I thought." Moma walks into her bedroom.

I go to the bathroom so I can cry like I want to. A soft knock sounds on the door. "Sis, you all right?" Junior, my brother asks through the door.

"Leave me alone, Junior."

"OK then."

I splash water on my face and pat my eyes. I go to my bedroom, ignoring Junior looking at me from his desk.

I close the door, *soft*. The last time I slammed it, they took the door off the hinges for two weeks. I didn't have no privacy or anything.

See, my folks are caught up in a time warp. They think this is the 1970's or something. All we got is rules, rules and more rules. This is what I mean:

- No dating until you are sixteen.

- No makeup until you are fifteen.

- Boys must walk to the door and meet your parents before a date.

- You will *not* walk out of that door if a boy blows for you.

109

-   If a boy wishes to date you, he must be here by 8 o'clock. You will *not* be treated as an afterthought.

-   If a boy visits at the house, he needs to be gone by 9 o'clock.

-   No house parties.

-   Do not tie up the phone. You can say everything you need to say in five minutes or less.

-   Do not call people before 8 a.m. nor after 9 p.m. This also applies to calls you receive.

-   Your curfew is 10 o'clock until you reach eighteen. Then your curfew is 12'o clock until you leave my house. I *don't care* if you are 30, it's still 12 o'clock!

-   Do not kiss or have a boy touching you in your parents' presence.

-   If you can't live with these rules, you are GROWN and need to move out.

See what I mean? Just unreasonable rules! They need to check the calendar. It's 2002! Things have changed. All that old-fashioned thinking gets on my nerves. They don't want us to have any fun!

No dates until I was sixteen. Why? All my friend girls started dating when they were thirteen or so. Their parent's don't even go with them. Why can't I do that? "Young people get into trouble dating too young and with no supervision," my Daddy says. Now what trouble can you get into going to the movies?

When I finally reached sixteen, they let me go to the school dance. I had to meet my date at the school. My Daddy said I was too young for boys to be picking me up. He brought me and sat outside in the car. I was too scared to slow dance and I had to tone down my fast dancing because I thought I saw him walking around in the gym. I didn't want him to come out on the dance floor and get me.

After a few months of this, they let finally let me go on a "real" date. I don't know *why* I even bothered. When my date arrived, my Daddy just "happened" to be sitting the living room cleaning his shotgun. My date stuttered so bad, my Daddy thought he was learning impaired. That boy never called me again.

Then you have the *fool* that drives up to my house at 11 p.m. My Daddy answered the door in his bathrobe and with his shotgun. I could have messed in my drawers when that boy asked for me! I swore I didn't know who it was. *Ignorant ass boy* 'bout got my ass tore up!

Now this here whipping was for no good reason at all. Petty mess.

See, I wanted to go to a house party over at my classmate's house. House parties are a BIG no, no as you can see from the list. My parents *hate* house parties.

They think all teenagers want to do is have sex. I begged and begged and finally they agreed to let me go to the party.

My Moma called her Moma to make sure there would be adults around. When she was satisfied with her Mom's answers, she said I could go. "Be home by ten o'clock!" Moma said. *Ten o'clock! That's when the party should just get jumping.* "You got a choice. Ten o'clock or stay home." I reluctantly agreed. I figured that once I was there, I might be able to call home and get some more time.

The party started getting crunked up around 9:30. Dang! I got to be home by 10. I decided to call home and ask if I could stay later. My Daddy answered and I asked him. He gave me a big, fat N-O. Shoot, I've got to leave now to get home in time. I decided to wait just a few more minutes.

Somebody decided to have a "Drop It Like It's Hot" contest. I *had* to watch this! Boy, them girls was *working* it! My Moma would have whipped the clothes off of me if I was dancing like that! Then this "sweet" boy in our class jumped on the floor wearing bikini swimming trunks and a tank top, dropped it, did a split and rolled around on the floor still in the split! We about tore the house down! You know he won. Hands down!

112

My friend girl's Moma walks up to me and says that my Moma just called. I'd better be getting on home. I glanced at my watch. Shit! It was 10:07. I took off out of the door like the police had stopped to offer me a ride. I ran all the way home. 10:14. I put my key in the lock quietly. Opened the door and shut it softly.

"Can you tell time?" I jumped a foot. My Daddy was standing behind the door. "Did your watch break?"

"No sir," I said. "I just miscalculated, that's all."

"Don't let me have to remind you again," he said, licking his lips. It's always a bad sign when he licks his lips.

"No sir, you won't." I heard my Moma coming down the stairs.

"What time did I tell you to be home, girl?"

"Ten o'clock."

"What time is it?"

"Ten seventeen."

"Bring your ass on over here." I see the belt in her hand. I'm too old for whippings!

"But, Moma…"

"Don't, but, Moma me," *Whap!*…..You know the rest.

I sigh and rub my sore behind. My parents' are wrong for treating me like this. I'm almost grown. Those psychologists on TV are right. It don't take all *these* rules to raise kids. Nosiree. There are better ways than this. Kids got feelings and stuff too.

Somebody's got to stop the madness and I'm gonna be the one! I'll show them how it's supposed to be done.

When I have kids, I ain't never gonna treat them like this. I'm not going to whup 'em, I'll just talk to them and use time-outs. I'm gonna let them date at 13 and go to parties and I'm gonna get them their own phone so they won't interfere with mine. I'll give them a curfew of 11:30 until they finish high school. If they need more time, we can negotiate it. After that, they can come and go as they please. I'm going to be with the times! Not stuck in 2002! I ain't gonna do none of that mess they did to me and my kids will be all right. I'll show them! Just wait!

ON THE DOWN LOW

I'm laying in bed snuggled up next to my girl. Sated.
A good, long love making session has put her to sleep.
I'm thinking of getting up to get a sandwich but I think
I'll wait a few more minutes.

Rrrrinngg!

Damn! Who is calling this time of night? I hurriedly
reach for the phone before it rings again and wakes up my
girl.

"Hello?"

"Motherfucker, you ain't *shit!* I bet you just finished
humping your *bitch*."

Oh shit. "Ah, how you doing?"

"This how you gonna play me?"

I glanced over at my girl. Good, she's still sleeping.
"Look, I'm busy right now, I'll holler at you tomorrow."

"Naw, motherfucker, you gonna *holler* at me *right
now!* You need to decide who is going to be 'The One'.
Either me or her."

"Why it gotta be like that?"

"It's *gonna* be like that because I *said* it's like that.
How 'bout I call chick tomorrow and tear your playhouse
down?"

"Alright. Alright. I'll let you know something tomorrow."

"One way or the other, motherfucker. You can't have it both ways." Click.

Shit! How this motherfucker gonna be sweating me at home knowing damn well my girl was over here. I'm changing my number tomorrow morning.

"Who was that?" my girl rolls over an asks.

"Just one of my boys, go back to sleep."

"What did he want?"

"He needed some money. I'll hook him up tomorrow."

"Oh," she rolls back over and is asleep in seconds.

I sit up the rest of the night trying to figure out what I am going to do. Hoping I can buy some time by changing my phone number; knowing it was just a patch on the problem, not the solution. But the truth would *devastate* my girl.

When morning finally arrives, I'm so wound up from no sleep, I can hardly take a shower and get dressed. I rush my girl, trying to get her out of the house. *You never can tell about people and I wasn't ready for no drama just yet.* I tell her I have to work late tonight, so I would catch her later in the week. Finally she leaves. I call the phone company and request a new private number. After taking care of that, I feel a little relieved, but not much and I head for work.

Blep. Blep. My office phone rings. "Hello."

"Did you decide yet?"

Damn! "Look, I really didn't appreciate you calling me last night. I told you my girl was coming over, so why'd you call?"

"I called because I'm *sick* of this lying and hiding and shit we doing."

"You knew the deal when we got together. Wasn't no lies."

"Well I'm *tired* of the old deal. This shit is whack. You love me, you love her, you love me, you love her. This is fucked up."

"Hey, if you feel like that, why don't we just call it quits and we can still be friends or whatever."

"It's like that, huh?"

"Yeah, it's like that."

"We'll *see*, motherfucka, we will see." Click.

Damn! I knew better than to get involved in some shit like this. I don't want to have to kill this fool, but I will. I *can't* let my girl know. But truth be told, I'm not ready to quit just yet. My manhood grows hard just thinking about the creeping I've been doing. That stuff is good. I've got to find a way to work this thing out.

117

Later that night, I'm still trying to find a solution when someone begins pounding on the door.

"Who is it?"

"Open this goddamn door!"

Here we go. I open the door, knowing what drama lies ahead, but I couldn't have my neighbors witnessing this shit.

"You changed your damn number, so I decided to come over. Where *is* she?"

"Calm down. She's not here. I was just about to call you."

"You a just-about-to-call-you lie. We gonna get this *shit* straight tonight."

"Look, just calm down." Shit, this motherfucker is looking good. Tight ass jeans and a cutoff T-shirt baring a lot of hairy chest. My member starts to rise. "I love you both. Why can't we just go on like we been doing?"

"There's other folks in the world. If you don't want to come clean, I'll just get to stepping."

"That's not what I want. I love you, you know that, and I want to make love to you. Here. Now."

"That's all you want to do. I'm looking for a full-time partner, not some part-time shit."

"Let me show you how much I care." I unsnap my jeans and unzip them, clearly showing my arousal. I remove my jeans, underwear and my shirt. Naked.

118

"Damn, man. I hate it when you do this to me."

"Get your shit off and let me love you."

The clothes are off in a flash. Mouth to mouth. Mouth to nipple. Hands pulling at my hair, pushing me down. Licking the arousal. Riding the man'gina.

I hear the key in the lock just as I reach my peak, but I can't stop. I hear the inhale of breath and I turn my head to see my girl standing in shock.

Watching me pumping into another man.

Seeing me cum.

Knowing I had been there before.

She doesn't say a word.

The switchblade is out and coming towards me before we can disentangle. She slices me from my right cheek to my stomach. As I was trying to get out of the way, she stabs my friend in the back twice. Blood is everywhere. She breaks a chair, picks up the leg and swings it at my head. I fend off that blow, but the kick to the privates doubles me over and she slams me over the head. I fall backwards towards the open door. I crawl outside and begin yelling for help. I keep hearing a thunk, thunk, thunk sound coming from inside. I hear the neighbor telling his wife to call 911, then mercifully, unconsciousness…

I awake in a hospital bed, wrapped from head to toe in bandage, feeling like a train had hit me and wondering what happened to my girl and my friend. The nurse comes in to change my bandage and I ask her what happened.

"What happened is that you are a very lucky man."

"How bad it is?"

"You were cut from face to abdomen. Your intestines had broken through the abdominal wall when the paramedics arrived. You just missed having your jugular vein cut. Say a prayer, because you are lucky to be alive."

"What happened to the other man and woman?"

"Here, let me let you read about it," she hands me a newspaper.

There on front page, in bold print for everybody and their Moma to see, the headlines "Love Triangle Results in Murder". My girl had beaten my friend's head in. When the paramedics arrived, she was steadily beating his head with the chair leg. *That must have been the thunk, thunk, thunk I had heard.* She has been charged with aggravated assault and murder. The court has her in a mental institution for evaluation. They say she hasn't spoken a word yet.

Damn! Damn! Damn! Now everybody knows.

I guess you know I don't receive many calls and my Moma can barely look at me when she visits. My sister asks me straight out how long I have been gay. I tell her

I'm not gay. I just got caught up in a situation too complex for her to understand. She told me they ought to neuter men like me. Going around fucking up women's lives. I was glad to see her go. I hear her call me a punk as she leaves.

My girl's folks call to tell me they hope I die. Yeah, me too.

When I finally get out, I have a notice from the company telling me they have downsized and my position is no longer there. The stuff from my office has been mailed to my house. I feel like I've been discriminated against and I want to sue, but I'm too embarrassed to tell a lawyer what has happened.

My money runs out before I'm well enough to find a job. I can't pay the rent, so I have to move. My mother tells me she prefers that I live somewhere else. I don't even *bother* to call my sister. My old friends either don't return my phone calls or tell me can't let me stay so, I put my stuff in storage, hoping I can get a job before the next month's rental is due.

I check into the Salvation Army hotel. Look into the old faces of young men. Hoping the unemployment checks will start soon so I can get out of this hell before I look like them. Get out of this life.

I save up four unemployment checks, buy a buy a bus ticket for clear across the country and start over. Once I arrive and find a job, I stay in the Salvation Army hotel until I receive my first check. Then I get an apartment. You don't need a car out here with all the public transportation and stuff.

Life is good. I've started dating again and already I've met this nice young lady that I like a lot. It's time for me to settle down, have some kids. This time I won't mess it up. I can't afford to mess it up...is that *fine* man winking at me?

I'VE BEEN LOVING YOU *TOO* LONG

The door slams and I breathe a sigh of relief. Finally, he's gone. At least eight hours all to myself. Rolling over slowly, I shuffle to the bureau and examine the damage: My eyes are black-rimmed like a raccoon; my hair is spiked all over my head, as if a dog got loose in it; and my left arm hangs lower than right. I shake my head to stop the parade of fist-handed images suddenly swimming behind my eyes.

Standing off-kilter somewhat, I manage to create the illusion that my shoulders are level, not wop-sided at all. Attempts to raise the left arm, causes pain to shoot from my fingers to my chest. I grope the bureau top to prevent myself from falling from the pain.

Why are you still here? the voice in my head asks me for the hundredth time. *Seems like as many times as I've asked you, you would have figured out a good explanation by now.*

I grasp the side of my head, my fingers curling around the blood-stiffened roots in my hand, trying to still the voice. When I can finally hear no more, I release the hair and cradle my arm. What am I supposed to do now? Makeup can't hide all this and Lord knows if I show up at the hospital with this arm and bruises all over my body, they're gonna pick Trey up at work and I can't afford to have them do that. Looking closely at myself, I suddenly realize that even though I'm only twenty-three, I could pass for forty.

Slumping on the bed, pain shoots up my arm and chest, causing tears to form in my eyes. Not able to stop them, they begin flowing freely onto my face, wetting my chest.

Stop crying and start packing! You sitting there and damn! you could be halfway to Mississippi by the time his sick ass gets off work.

I cry out in frustration as the voice continues harassing me.

Ain't no white knight gonna come and rescue your ass, you got to do it yourself. Get to moving!

I *can't* leave! Where in the world will I go? With what? They don't let you ride on promises. It's cash, grass or ass or you can keep on stepping. Since I don't have the first two and Trey would kill me if I did the last, I'm stuck.

Bullshit! You stuck 'cause you want to be stuck. Anyway, after last night, can't you tell Trey gonna kill your ass sooner or later anyway? Leave!

"*I...can't...leave!*" I yell to the empty room. Trey needs someone to help him. He can't cook for himself

124

and you know how he does the laundry. He'll be walking around here looking like a clown or something if I didn't take care of that. He *needs* me.

Trey needs a good beat down that's all he needs. Don't you worry, Trey will find another "victim" and bump her head good, like he did yours. Trey don't need you!

My heart clutches as I contemplate that I could be replaced. Trey *loves* me. He won't be able to find another person to care for him and take care of him like I do. I know this and...

What damn planet you living on? You must be looking at "America's Dysfunctional Home Videos". People who love you don't whip your ass like you slapped their newborn baby up sides the head. Girl, ain't no loving going on up in here, unless you the one doing it.

"Stop it!" I yell out. Why is my mind doing this? Every time Trey and I have a "love spat", the voices in my head try to turn me against him. Try to get me to leave, knowing good and well that nobody can love me like Trey. A small smile pushes onto my lips as I stroll down memory lane...

I met Trey when we in the eight grade—me, the new girl and him, the "Big Man" in our grade. I remember how all the girls snubbed me until I hooked this fine fellow they all wanted. Stuck up heffas. I showed them. I lucked out *big time*.

We started courting slowly— talking during Break, eating lunch together and finally going to the Jr. High dance together. When we went to the dance together, those other girls just gave up. Wasn't no hope for them anymore. I had him and he had me and we were giggling happy.

Our relationship only deepened throughout high school. The courting turned into hand-holding, then petting and finally I let him be my "first." We were happy—he wanted to marry me before we even finished. I guess I would have if my Daddy hadn't told us no.

College is when things got funny. The guys at college kept walking up and talking to me and since I'm polite, as well as friendly, I didn't see a thing wrong with it. Trey did though. The first time he saw me talking, he grabbed my arm so tight, he left a bruise in the imprint of his fingers. At first, I was mad as hell! Don't nobody grab on me! My roommate just laughed though. She said, "Girl, he's just jealous. He must *really* love you, if he's acting like that." That makes sense.

When he saw this guy pull on my shirt, he walked up and grabbed my arm and took me behind the dorm so we could talk. I could see the jealous *love* in his eyes and my heart soared. He *really* loves me! The slap he hauled off and gave me shocked me. I told him never to speak to me again! I had to tussle with him to get back into the dorm! My roommate just laughed at me. "Girl, that was just a little 'love tap.' Let him suffer for a few days and go on and make up. Y'all been together too long to break up 'cause he gave you a little slap." This made sense.

Trey came back before dinner—throwing rocks at my window to get my attention, almost breaking the pane. I ignored him, until finally he snuck up the back stairs and knocked on my door. That he risked getting put out of school to reconcile with me, just made me melt. He *loves* me. I *know* it.

Things were on a roller coaster ride for the next two years— first he's mad and hitting me and the next day he's repentant and sorry. By this time, I didn't even look at other guys. I just kept my head down, not speaking to anybody. They called me "stuck up" and said I thought I was "too good for them", but if that's what it took to keep Trey happy, too bad.

When we finished college, I thought we would move away, get good jobs, and we'd get married. We did moved away and since we were away from any of our family and "grown", we decided to move in together.

We had a nasty fight when I got offered a better paying job than he did, though. That's the day when Trey told me he was from the "old school." Wasn't no woman of his gonna be working. All I needed to do was keep the house clean, have a good hot meal waiting on him when he got home and he would bring home the "cheese".

I turned to *mush*. He *loves* me! Do you hear me? This man *loves* me! Nobody else would even *suggest* trying to get out there and hustle so their woman could stay home. I agreed and I showed him how much I appreciated him later on that night.

Somehow, though, something in me always made me keep messing up! Either I cooked the grits too soupy or there was a spot on his shirt or the house was junky or I wasn't finished with dinner when he came home... something! This just made him mad as hell and he moved from just slapping and shaking me to hitting me with his fists. I tried harder and harder to please him, but no matter what, I just kept fucking up and he kept fucking me up.

Frustrated, I told him I was leaving 'cause I felt like he didn't love me like he said he did. Well, this sure showed him. He was scared every time he left out the door— begging me to be there when he got home from work; buying me lingerie and candy and stuff. Besides, who would help him? He couldn't take care of himself all by *himself*?

I let him stew for a few days. Let him wonder whether I would be "poof" when he walked in the door or not.

The voices in my head started talking to me then. They told me to *Go! Get out! Find someone better!* I could see the *love* in his eyes every time he came in the door and saw me, though— apprehension replaced by relief, once he ferreted me out in the apartment. I guess he still wasn't convinced because he finally walked in with a big, fat engagement ring. That did it for me and I slammed the door on those meddling voices, trying to get me to leave my man. I *know* he loves me!

Things got back on track after that. I was beginning to get bored with this "Suzy Homemaker" routine, but he seemed happy, so I kept going. We had our differences, like all couples do, but he only slapped me and shook me. He didn't *dare* hit me with his fists! That is, not until last night...

I had cooked fried chicken, his favorite. The table was set, the house was freshly vacuumed and I was folding clothes when he walked in. I knew he was looking kind of funny when he walked in, but I thought that he was just under stress from some office mess. He didn't say a word as he took off his coat and tie. He undid the buttons on his cuff, then walked over to me and backhanded me into the refrigerator!

"Who you been seeing, bitch?!" he screamed into my face.

Seeing? What is he talking about?! "Nobody!" I screamed back.

"Oh, you seeing somebody," he said as he grabbed my hair.

"I'm not! I've been with you and only you since..."

"You just a lie!" He snatched my head towards his face. "If you been with only me, then how did I get this case of VD I got?"

Venereal disease? What is he talking about? "But...I...but..." I blubbered, confused.

"You think I'm gonna be out there busting my ass everyday so you can lay around with any motherfucker you want? *And* your dumb ass gave me VD on top of it?" The spittle from his lip flies into my eyes. "Well, that ain't gonna happen. I'll kill your skinny ass 'graveyard dead', before that happens!"

I hold up my hands, pleadingly, "Trey, I have *never* cheated on you! I don't know about no VD or whatever you say you got, but I didn't give it to you!"

"Yes you did. Some punk you been fucking gave you gonorrhea and now you gave it to me!" His fingers move from my hair to the collar of my shirt, cutting off my air.

I struggle, in an attempt to get some oxygen in my bursting lungs. Flinging my arms; pounding on his chest. He slaps me to the floor. As I look up at him, his booted foot connects with my armpit. *Why is he doing this? I*

130

haven't been with no man! Maybe it was the new douche I've been using? I did have a yeast infection last week, maybe that's what it is.

I curl into a fetal position as his hands and feet meet my flesh again and again. Finally, with a final glob of spit I feel crawling down my neck, the attack stops. Arms cradle me. Lift me and take me to the bedroom. A warm towel wipes the spittle from my neck and is placed over my throbbing head. A kiss is placed on my cheek followed by, "I'm sorry. But, we'll get through this. I don't know why you did this, but we'll work it out."

The voices emerge from my brain as the bedroom door closes. *You ready to go? When he leaves in the morning, get you shit and let's go!*

Leave me alone! This is just a little misunderstanding.

The only misunderstanding here, is me misunderstanding why you hadn't dialed 9-1-1. That fool almost killed you! What more do you need?

Shut up! He *loves* me!

That motherfucker don't "love" nothing but whipping your ass!

Shut...up! I don't want to think about this right now. My head is killing me and my body aches all over. I think my arm is dislocated. So, please *Shut Up*! Now!

I'm gonna shut up for now, but you know that "loving" motherfucker could have at least brought you a Motrin or something.

I squeeze my eyes shut and blissfully, sleep claims me...

Bringing myself back to the present, I painfully push myself back to sitting position. I stare in the mirror, wondering who that jacked up woman is starring back at me.

How many heel prints it's gonna take before we go? What? You got to see that 'bright light' and some angels floating around before you believe me?

Trey's just made a mistake. I haven't been with anybody, so there is no way he can have gonorrhea. It's just a mistake, that's all.

Girl, if you don't get that phone book and look up a shelter, I'm gonna jump out your head and beat your ass myself!

Shelter? I'm not going to no shelter. Things are not nearly that bad.

Trust me. They are. Anyway, what would it hurt to talk to somebody down there? They might be able to give you some good advice since you don't want to believe your own common sense.

I don't need to talk to no shelter!

Okay. If you won't talk to a shelter, why don't you get up and get yourself tested for VD? If he says he got it, then you probably do too. And if you didn't give it to him, then...

What you saying? It *ain't* no other woman, 'cause Trey would *never* cheat on me! He *loves* me!

I didn't say that. Just take a shower, throw a cap on your head, put on some sunglasses and go down to the Health Department and get tested. It should only take a day or two before you know something.

Hmmm. That makes sense. Then Trey can see that this has all been a bad mistake. I don't have VD, so he can't.

It was an ordeal to take the shower and get dressed. Since my head was still pounding, I gingerly sat a cap on it, before pulling on my sunglasses. Catching a bus to the Health Department, I was glad to claim a seat to myself. If someone jostled my hurt arm, I might have started crying right there.

The Health Department people looked at me strangely, but they quickly got the samples and told me to call in the following day. I didn't really care since I knew that the test would be negative, but I took the card they offered anyway.

Returning home, I realized that I had only an hour or two before Trey arrived and I forgot to take any meat out

133

of the freezer for dinner. Suddenly panicked, I frantically think about what to do. Trey has *got* to eat when he gets home, otherwise his night goes bad.

Fuck Trey! What you gonna be eating with that fat lip of yours?

I push the voice down into the deep recesses of my brain. I know! I'll order in food. Claiming the telephone directory, I quickly locate the Chinese food place he loves and order his dinner.

Trey enters the apartment in good spirits, a large bouquet of flowers in his hands.

"What are the flowers for?" I ask .

"For being a fool. I shouldn't have hit you like I did. I was just upset and…I guess my bladder was acting up and I thought…you had been fooling around on me or something," he lowers his eyes and looks repentant. "You are the best thing to come into my life. I can't imagine life without you. I don't just love you, I *love* you." He holds out the bouquet, "You are my beautiful flower and these are for you."

Oh. I can't help the warm feeling that flows from my head to my feet.

Girl, that man don't love *you. Can't you see that he is just setting you up for the next time he*…I deadbolt the corner of my mind I send the voice to this time.

"Trey, I love you too. I know you were just upset, but like you said we can work through this misunderstanding."

"You not going to leave me?" I see the fear in his eyes.

"No." Relief returns to his face. "I've been loving you this long and I plan to love you until the end of time."

"Oh, thank you, *Jesus*, for another chance," he says and places a kiss on my cheek. I wince from the pain and he sees this. "Oh, I forgot. I picked you up some antibiotics and stuff."

"What kind?"

"It's some penicillin. You've got to take a lot of them, but once you do, the swelling and pain will leave faster and you will be good as new in a week or so."

"Penicillin is for pain?"

"No. It's for the swelling. I don't want you to get an infection or anything from the swelling."

That makes sense. "How many I got to take."

"Well, you need a big dose, so they suggested twelve."

"One or two a day or what?"

"No. All at once."

"You sure?"

"Baby, I love you and I wouldn't do anything to kill you."

135

I struggle, but I manage to get all 12 of the Penicillin capsules down my throat. "That was nasty!" I exclaim.

"Well, if you didn't take them, the infection would be worse. Hey, I've been thinking, let's go ahead and set the wedding date."

"You mean it?!" I yell excitedly.

"Yes. I want you to be with me forever, until the end of our days."

Bliss overtakes my body. See, I told you he *loves* me! Those stupid voices. I'm never listening to them again. I lean into his tender hug, throwing the card, with the Health Department number on it, in the trash can behind his back.

We won't be needing *that* anymore!

NO REST FOR THE WEARY

The rumbling of the garage door rising jolts me into action. I grab my cap and shut off the television. As I hear the car rolling into its space, I open the back door and exit silently, trot-walking as fast as I can towards the tool shed in the backyard. Hearing the interior door open, I fumble with the handle of the shed, dart inside and quickly close the door with a quiet "click". Leaning on the door, I refuse to move a muscle, lest I bush against some tool and she hears me.

Damn! It's hot in here! I stare into the gloomy recesses of the shed as sweat collects under my hat. A mosquito, trapped inside without a decent blood meal for days, alights on my neck and bites me. Slapping at the annoying insect, I upset a rake, which commences to clatter noisily as it hits the floor. The neighbor's dog, whose dog house is, unfortunately, located just behind this shed, begins its barking. Clawing at the fence and barking incessantly. Glancing quickly out the window, I see her opening the rear door. Looking around, she settles her gaze on the shed.

"Daddyyyy. Daddyyyy, are you out there?" she calls in sing-song.

I cringe at the sweet endearment. Twenty years ago, heck five years ago, my heart lifted with joy when she called me Daddy. Now, it's just a precursor to trouble. She wants some. Now.

Hearing the screen door slam, I see her rapidly approaching the shed. Hastily, I shove the large trashcan to the side and shimmy into the vacated space. I squeeze my old, tired body into a space big enough for a little boy, twisting my head uncomfortably to the side, trying to hide my body fully.

The door opens. "Daddy, you out here?" she says. I can hear her dress material swishing as she walks around. I hold my breath, afraid that an inhalation or exhalation might be just loud enough for her to hear. One of the mosquito's siblings takes this opportunity to light and I am powerless to stop its blood meal. Poor mosquito. It'll probably be just as tired as I am once it drinks my weary blood.

I hear her steps receding and the door closing. I remain in my cramped hiding space until I hear the screen door slam again. Finally, I struggle to relieve my screaming muscles. Finding that I am unable to stand, I roll out onto the floor and pull myself up using the table saw for support. Looking down at myself, I am mad and embarrassed. Dirt and litter cover my lower pant legs and my knees and back ache from the awkward position I placed myself in.

Fifty years old and hiding from my wife like I'm a bad child. Shoot!

I love my wife. I really do, but something has happened to her. I don't mean something harmful, but...I don't really know what it is, but its *something*. See, we've been married twenty years. Twenty *good* years. Got through the kids and now we sitting pretty headed for retirement. I love her just as much as I did when I said "I do." I'm a little bit older than she is, but that's not the problem either. It's just that lately she wants to give me some all the time. Morning, noon and night. Damn near every time she steps in the door, she wants me to get my Johnson ready for her. I swear I got "strawberry" burns on my rod from all the sex. She acts like we just got married!

Just a few months ago, I was content to get me some loving maybe two or three times a month. Keep the plumbing going, if you know what I mean. Now... now its BAM! BAM! BAM! Like she went back in time or something. I was excited the first two or three weeks, but now I'm just plumb tired of it all.

I want to say this whole "new her" started after she went to a bachelorette party for one of her sorority sisters. She told me how much fun she had and about the male stripper that performed for them. I wasn't mad or anything. She can look just like I can, but she knows where her bacon come from. Next thing I know, she's become a wildcat in a pantyhose. Bought some flicks and wanted to try out some new positions. Shoot, she damn near bought out that Victoria Secretions store in the mall—new panties and bras and some other things I don't know *what* you wear them for.

I worked with her. I figured she was having a mid-life crisis and all. She could have gone out and had an affair with a younger man, like a lot of women do. But instead she just revved up my engine and just about shot the pistons on this old jalopy.

I'm not saying I don't want to get some from my wife, I'm just saying I don't want to get *so much* from her. Don't get me wrong, ain't nothing wrong with her! I've got no reason to complain. She's hasn't gained more than ten pounds since I married her and she keeps her hair and nails together. A lot of men envy me. I see them looking at her out of the corner of their eyes when we are together. Wanting what I got. Just keep wanting, chumps.

When I finally starting getting tired of this sexual overdose, I tried to cut back politely. I told her I had to work on some office projects at home or I needed to do some things around the house...any old excuse. At one point, I got so pitiful, I told her I had a headache. I shudder remembering that moment.

She wasn't hearing none of that mess, though. Next thing I know she talking about getting me some of them Viagra pills. I told her I didn't need no Viagra. Ain't nothing wrong with my Johnson! She seemed to relent. Started having my coffee ready for me just a soon as I stepped out of the shower and she hadn't done that for me in years. You know, before I could finish the cup of coffee, I could feel my Johnson rising to attention. Hard attention. She just hopped on it and had herself a good time. Well... I admit I did too. But, once she finished, it seemed to take forever for my stuff to soften up. It stayed hard for an hour or more.

I wasn't too concerned. I just thought I was getting back into my old style, you know? Then I heard her on the phone telling one of her sisters that she crushed up a Viagra pill every morning and put it into my coffee and now she gets all she wants any day she wants it. I stopped drinking coffee that day. I told her I was cutting back and switching to milk. Cold milk.

Did that stop her? No. She just switched to new tactics—grabbing me when I changed clothes from work, whenever she caught me getting into and out of the shower. I mean, my Johnson was in danger of being ripped from my body! I tried to stay up later than she did

141

and hop in bed when she was asleep. I even took some old clothes with me to work and changed there. No go. She's still humping me every time she wants to and I'm just plain tired, weary and drained.

Fifty years old and afraid to go in the house. My house that I'm paying on. Ugh oh, here she comes again. I hear my old bones cracking as I squat back into my hiding place.

The door opens. "Daddy, now you can just come out from over there behind the trash can. I saw you when I came in here the first time. What you doing over there hiding anyway?" she says.

I'm caught now! Frustrated, I kick the trash can from in front of me and grip the saw as I reluctantly rise.

"Look at you. Dirt all over your pants...what you doing over there?" she questions me, her eyes narrowed.

"Uh...uh...I dropped something and I was trying to get at it and I got stuck," I reply lamely.

"You been over there since I first came out here?"

"Yeah. Like I said, I was trying to get something that fell under the table and got stuck."

"Oh. I thought you was trying to hide from me. You know, playacting and all. Shoot, I thought we were playing Hide And Go Seek and you wanted me to look for you," she finishes with a laugh. "Look what I put on so you could Hide and Go Seek on me."

142

With that, she flings open the robe I just realized she was wearing. Neon pink shimmery lacy bra and panties are revealed. Oh no, not again!

"What you think? I just picked it up at the mall. You like it?"

"I love them." What? You think I'm stupid or something?

"I knew you would that's why I bought them," she says reaching out a hand to me. I take it like a man about to be hanged and she is the executioner. Wrapping her arms around me, she says, "Come on back into the house. I'm ready to break these panties in, know what I mean?"

Gulping, because unfortunately I do, I paste a false smile on my lips, all the while glancing around the shed looking for something to claim I needed to finish. Seeing nothing, I finally say, "I know."

"How about the bathroom in the other bedroom? We've never done it there. I was thinking I could hop on the vanity and you could just stand in front of me..."

My mind goes blank as she drags me across the back yard, continuing to describe, in detail, what she plans for us to do. Numb, she leads me through the door...

Help me. Please...somebody help...me...

MERCY KILLING

My son holds onto my arms tightly as we walk down the aisle of the church. I refuse to look right or left at the people standing and staring in the pews. The music drones on softly as the preacher loudly proclaims the Scriptures. Finally reaching the front pew, I slide towards the inside as my son moves in besides me. The preacher, his back ram-rod straight in his quest to fulfill his last rite duties, rises into the pulpit and the organ music ceases.

I finally gaze at the object of all this attention— my husband's coffin. Center aisle. In the spotlight for the last time. Well, Buddy, the fat lady finally sung and she's sitting right here in this pew.

Loud crying draws my eyes from the coffin and across the aisle. *I cannot believe this shit here!* There she is sitting on the front row, sniffing like *her husband* died with all them crumbsnatchers crying along with her. I bristle in spite of the occasion. Ignoring the preacher's speech, I stare at this tramp. This *other woman* who has the *nerve* to be up in my home church crying like she's got a right to. Bitch.

Staring hard at the casket, I wish I could get my hands on my husband's lying cheating, pumping heart just one more time. Oh! If his ass wasn't already dead, I would kill him again. The tears begin to stream down my face. Lying, cheating, two-faced asshole. I've been loving you since I was thirteen and now your floozy up in here like she belongs and ain't nobody did nothing. Gave her a front row seat. The folks must be just tittering like crazy.

The loud, mournful wailing emitting from his floozy, makes me lift out of my seat. Hatred creates a red haze over my corneas. No *she ain't* gonna be up in here acting like this! I'm gonna snatch a knot in her ass so tight, they will have to cut off her legs to unravel it.

My son pulls at my arms, wraps his arms around me and presses my head into his shoulder. "Shush, Mama. I'm here. It's gonna be all right," he says.

I look into the tear-streaked face of my baby and realize that he thinks I'm overcome with grief. *Baby if you only knew.*

I settle myself into his arms, still wishing I could kill his sorry ass daddy one more time. I stare daggers at the casket. Bad enough your sorry ass left your desk open and I found the life insurance policy leaving her $250,000 and me only $50,000. Then you messed up and missed the car payment on her Infiniti and the company calls when you are out to find out when you would be making the next payment. To top it all off, you, with your usual lack of imagination, hide the deed to the beachfront condo you purchased for her and your *crumbsnatchers*

145

between the mattresses of the guest bedroom. Don't you know I'm the one who changes the sheets around here? Asshole. *Did you enjoy the last grits I served you up? I sure hope you did, cause I enjoyed watching you falling to the floor, gasping for air and clutching your chest.*

Childhood friends hop up to the microphone to proclaim what a good friend, husband and provider my husband was. Please! That jerk was taking food out of my children's mouths for his tramps. Just as soon as I ended one of his affairs, he started another one. I could hardly live decently! Then he goes and gives the world to this...this...*whore*. Finally, they sit down. Good damn thing too. I was just about to tell them to quit telling lies about that dirty dog I married.

The Funeral Director moves to the front to open the casket for the last viewing. The people stream by, some sniffing, others nodding quietly. I paste a pitiful smile on my face as I receive condolence after condolence.

I stare past the mourners shoulders as his *tramp* shuffles her brood towards the open casket. The children cry out loudly in grief, "Daddy! Daddy! Don't leave us Daddy!" and I shrink in my seat. The church seems too quiet all of a sudden. As the ushers help the children to their seats, *she* just stands there crying loudly. In horror, I watch as she reaches out to stroke his face and chest, telling the world she had been with my husband. She

146

leans into the casket, murmuring something I couldn't hear, all the while continuing to stroke his chest.

Suddenly, I see movement further down his body, just at the point where the lower door intersects the body. *What in the world is that? I know she isn't running her hands under his clothes is she?* But glancing upwards, I see her hands are still stroking his face and chest.

The movement continues until it peaks high and tall beyond the rim of the casket. *I know damn well this isn't what I think it is.* I struggle forward towards the casket. My son lurches from his seat to assist me. I push his floozy aside to settle myself at the casket. I stare hard at the protrusion in the casket, my mind refusing to believe what my eyes are telling me is true. *Now you son of a bitch! You dead and about to go to your grave and you still getting a hard on for this heffa!* The disbelief yields to utter fury. This motherfucker is dead and still getting it up for her?! *You no good asshole, you!*

With superhuman strength, I reach into the coffin and grab a good, solid handful of his suit coat and lift his dead, cold, hard body out of the coffin. I intended to drag him out on the street so the Sanitation Department could pick his ass up like the dog he was.

My son, stunned by my actions, just stands there staring at me. The Funeral Director and ushers grab at my arms, but I punch furiously, not caring whose face my fists connect with.

His floozy decides to get into the act. "Stop it!" she yells, pulling at my arms. *Oh, she wants a piece of me, I see.* I snatch her shoulders and pull that heffa down across the body. She finally stops her tumble kneeling at his crouch.

"What's wrong with you!" she yells.

"You been down there before, so what's the goddamn problem *now*?!" I yell back, stomping his chest (and breaking off my shoe heel) for good measure. I kick at the offending protrusion, hoping I could break his dick off and stuff it into her open mouth.

The preacher has rushed from the pulpit and is now speaking quickly and calmly by my side. I don't want to hear what he has to say though. As I grab a leg, intending to drag this womanizing trash to the street, more arms engulf me. I throw my head backwards, intending to bust whoever's lip is in the way. With a grunt, arms release me, but others converge and pull me to the floor. Face to face with this lying fucker I married. Right next to the bitch he was fucking to the end.

I yell out ugly, nearly incoherent things to his sewn-close eyes. I spit in his cold, hard face as I wiggle, subdued, on the floor. Rough hands lift and push me onto a pew. A line of men with disbelief, horror and anger

148

etched into their faces, stand in front of me, blocking my way.

The Funeral Director and his crew begin lifting the body back into the casket. Rearranging the clothes and repositioning the legs and hands. They hurriedly close the lid, afraid I would desecrate this..this *garbage* any further. The legs of the casket gurney are unlocked and they begin rolling it towards the door.

The years of humiliation give me the strength to surge forward and I push the men backwards. "Stop!" I yell. As the Funeral Director turns to me, expecting another outburst, I stare at the coffin, then back at him. Finally I say, "Burn him. Don't waste a drop of precious ground on this...*dog.* Incinerate his ass!"

"Moma! What are you doing?!" my son cries out. The gasps and disbelief of the congregation are heard and dismissed. *They didn't say shit when she was up there trying to get her groove on in the casket, now did they?*

Turning towards his sorrowful face, I say, "Son, I'm sorry, but... I'm the next of kin and I want his ass cremated."

His other children begin crying out, "Don't burn up my Daddy! Don't burn up my Daddy!"

The Funeral Director, his face a study in horror, finds his voice, "Ma'am, you are just upset. This is what you arranged— burial in the church's cemetery."

149

"I know what I said before, but now I want him cremated." *His ass just doesn't want to lose the difference in money. Fuck him.*

Staring at my son, whose pleas fall on my deaf ears, the Funeral Director nods his head and slowly rolls the casket forward.

Not trusting him or the rest of the family, I give a parting threat. "Do what I say now or I'll have your license yanked before the dirt cools on this casket." The Funeral Director stiffens his back and barks out the order to return the body to the Funeral Home.

I ignore the stunned faces of the folks who think I've lost my mind. My son shrinks from me, refusing to aid me on my walk back down the aisle. So what. A smile tugs at the corner of my mouth, thinking about how I finally gave this mangy dog his comeuppance.

Stepping into the sunlight, my heart fills with joy as I watch them load the casket into the hearse. *Won't nobody be coming to bring you flowers. You'll just be up on the mantle looking at me living, wishing for the umpteenth time you could have been better to me. You don't keep messing over a woman and never expect to get yours. You know payback is a mother—*

"Ma'am, would you come with us?"

I turn to see two police officers with hands extended towards me. One nods his head towards a patrol car with the engine running, the rear door open.

"What? This has all been a big misunderstanding. The things that man did to me while we were married...I just snapped...and I don't think it's a crime to go off like I did."

"That not the crime. Ma'am, you are under arrest for the murder of your husband." One of the policemen says, holding out a piece of paper for me.

"That's not possible. I didn't kill him...he died of a heart attack."

"Not according to the Medical Examiner's report. Your husband died of strychnine apparently administered in his grits. Will you follow us Ma'am?"

I look back at the folks standing on the steps watching the whole ordeal unfold. His hussy grasping her children's hands; my son with eyes big as saucers. You would have thought Gabriel had blown his trumpet the way they stood so still. No one comes forward to intercede on my behalf.

Turning back to the officers, I nod my head and walk quietly to the patrol car. Settling myself into the back seat, I lean out before they close the door and yell to the Funeral Director, "This doesn't change a thing! Burn his ass up good and flush the ashes!"

As the car rolls out of the parking lot, I begin to laugh loudly, the tears streaming down my face. *Well, well, well, dear husband. You should have paid attention to the old folk's saying: 'If I can't have you, then nobody will!'*

Concerned, the policemen look back as I begin to laugh even louder, laying down the foundation for my insanity plea. I slam my head against the window as we continue down the road, laughing hysterically all the while. I should be worried but I'm not. Afterall, everybody knows that if a woman kills her man, he just about *needed* killing.

SOMEWHERE IN AMERICA

Well, well, well. It's a glorious morning to be alive! Me, Mamie Louella Willis, eighty-eight and still kicking. I ain't kicking high, but I'm still kicking. I stretch my arms up to the ceiling, thankful for another day. Getting out of bed takes a little work when you get old. I can tell that Mr. Arthritis done already made his daily deposit as I reach down to rub my knee to ease some of the pain. My belly is so big, I can't see them knees anymore. Long heavy breasts sit in my lap like dough, warming my skinny thighs. *Time is hell on a body.*

Get up, old girl!

I heave my plump rump up out of the bed. I limp down to the kitchen and fix me a hot toddy—coffee with plenty of E&J. I gots to get me a pick-me-up early in the morning. Besides, everybody knows a hot toddy will stop you from getting colds and will clear up them sinuses.

I flip on the TV. Let me see what happened since last night. Murder. Rape. Burglary. Them folks protesting about fur again. Same ole, same ole. Ain't nothing new that hadn't been news before. When you've lived as long as I have, you seen it all, done it all.

I've been living on this same street nearly half a century. The names change, but the folks are still the same. You got the messy folks you stay away from, the bourgeois folks that don't associate with anybody, the really nice folk and the be-like-the-Jones folks. It's a regular keeping-up-shit-show right here. Somebody needs to call Jerry. He ain't seen nothing!

Look, there's Miss Johnson with her new baby. *When she gonna quit having them chaps?* That gal ain't got a lick of sense in that big old pumpkin head of hers. Man in, man out. She needs a notebook to keep up with all the last names of them kids. You would think that as much as she is up in that Divine One somethinganother church, she would know fornicating is a sin by now.

Now she says she gon' marry a man in prison. Says he doing time for a murder he didn't commit. DNA test lied and everything. They didn't lie on them men she got them children by, did they? Hhump! All the men walking around that been up in her snatch and she gonna marry a jailbird? I just *know* she ain't gonna have that man come to live with her children when he gets out, is she? Always knew she was a Loony Toon.

Here comes her friend from church to pick her up. What *is* that gal's name? Well...I remember when she was just knee-high to a rabbit. Her folks were some *good*, church folks. They raised her right! I know it!

Now she running around town giving up her cookie talking about some "healing love" she learned about at the church.

Somebody please tell that girl she's a 'ho! Black, white, yellow or red. Ain't no discrimination there. She just turning tricks for no money.

I tried to talk some sense to her. Told her that she'd better be careful, there's plenty of stuff out there you can catch that will kill you. Gave her a STD pamphlet out of my Bible bag. She *needed* it!

Do you know that gal started misquoting scriptures saying that "healing love" is all right. Says her pastor released her from bondage and it was her duty to spread the good news. I just shook my head. They say the pastor's wife heard about her "healing experience" and threatened to whip her ass in the church parking lot. I sho' hate I missed service that day.

There's that boy who dresses up like a gal with his "friend." *His friend was the one mixed up in that flip-flop love triangle.* I guess he knows he all the way flipped, 'cause they suppose to get married next month. That poor girl he was dating, in his "other" life, still up in the sanitarium. Ain't said two words, they say. Just a mess.

Looks like they been out jogging. He says he got to keep in shape 'cause *his men* don't like all that flab and stuff hanging out. I tell you one thing, he is ugly as homemade sin but he sho' is a *sharp* dresser. Shit, he's got more clothes than any woman I know. Must be custom made, the way they fit him. I wonder where he gets shoes to fit them big old feet?

Gots plenty of money by the looks of it, too. He supposedly owns that new nightclub, The Bushy Hole, up on 5th Street next to that Divine church. They say you can't tell if you are talking to a man or a woman up in there.

Chile, I was up in Butcheros just last week getting me a blue rinse for my hair, and in he comes like he owns the joint. Told Pauleon he didn't want to *hear* no *shit* about no *appointment*. He needed his hair done up right away! He was in a *snit*!

I overheard him telling Pauleon he got into a fight with some cashier up at the W&P about some ketchup. What the hell he fighting about ketchup for?

Oh gracious me, they *kissing* on the street!

You know, I tried to help that boy when he first moved here. I snuck over while he was at work and put a green Bible in his mailbox. I put some church pamphlets about the sin of "alternative lifestyles" in his door. Guess he threw them all out 'cause I know for a fact, he cussed out the Jehovah witness folks when they came to his door early one Saturday morning. Just heathen. Anyway, I'm gonna have to talk to him though. Kissing men on the streets ain't good for the children to see. Mixes up their minds and all. Umm, umm, umm.

Oh there's Mrs. Keeping-Up-With-The-Joneses herself. Guess she must be off today. She gets on my last ass telling me about what she bought, how much this costs, where her husband is taking her on vacation and where she sends her kid to school and all.

There's trouble in paradise though. Last month, she came flying out of her house all wild-eyed and just about ran over me while I was out walking Pookie. I almost had a coronary right there!

Pete, the mailman, said her husband was served child support papers. *I sho' hope it wasn't Miss Johnson's kid.* They say she put him out. Miss Johnson and her friend called themselves going over there to pray for them. I heard the cussing and yelling all the way up the street to my house! Well, I guess they must be working things out, since he still there. He don't act the same though.

I look down the street at the huge house they just built in the cul-de-sac. The man that built that house came in here and bought the old house where that woman killed her husband with some poisoned grits, and tore it down. Paid *cash* for it, they say!

Being neighborly and all, I asked him what he did for a living. Now you ain't gonna believe this. He says he is a *janitor*. He got a new BMW, fat gold chains and wears them Armando or somebody suits. What they paying janitors now? Must be a chain of janitor businesses. He gave one of his business cards. I couldn't find him in the phone book and none of my friends ever *heard* of his business. I'll bet he's a drug dealer.

A moving van pulls up to the house across the street. Uhmm umph. That girl has put on some weight! I remember when she moved into that house with her boyfriend, must have been ten years ago. She started popping them kids right out. I don't know why they didn't get married. She kept saying things were good and she didn't want to mess it up. I could see in her eyes she was lying though. I heard 'em yelling. She wanted to and he didn't.

Then her boyfriend gets hisself killed in a car wreck. Chile, I'm telling you, his folks showed out in the street the day after the funeral! Told her she had to get out, cause they was going to sell the house. See he had credit life and the house was paid off. His Moma told her she didn't care *where* she stayed as long as it wasn't there.

That girl asked his Moma about the insurance money. His Moma told her if he didn't leave her none, she ain't got none...I'm gonna miss that girl.

I walk up to the corner drug store for some liniment before my stories come on, just enjoying the day. Is that Mabel Lee's daughter? I didn't know she worked here.

That gal has let herself go all to hell! Hair needs a perm, she got "dunlap" disease *(stomach done lapped over the top of her pants)*, and she looks hard. Tsk. Tsk. Tsk. That girl had so much promise. *Smmaarrt*! We just *knew* she was going to be a doctor or an engineer or something.

I told Mabel Lee, when I seen that slick grown ass man sniffing up behind that gal, wasn't no good in him. I knowed he was married. Didn't do no good. That gal was pregnant before we knew anything. I don't think she even finished high school.

She's got her hands full with that son of hers and working. People say that snake she had the baby by keeps moving so he won't pay child support. Pitiful.

I get my liniment and walk back home, passing that gal wearing a turtleneck and dark glasses again, like we don't know what's going on. Why else would you have on a turtleneck in 90+ degree weather? Ain't that much loving in the world for me!

I wave at the new couple that moved in a few months ago. Boy, she keeps herself pretty as a picture, but her husband knows he looks tired all the time. The other day, I was out feeding Pookie in the backyard, and I saw him running to the shed in their backyard just as she was getting home. He was moving like the police were at the door. I sure hope he ain't smoking crack or nothing back

159

there. Pookie was barking at that shed like something funny was going on though.

I notice a big Lincoln Continental with BLSZNGS on the license plate, parked in Miss Bourgeois-Don't-Even-Speak-To-Me-If-You-Ain't-Rich's house. Is that Deacon Myers coming out of her house? What is he doing over here? *She ain't got on nothing but a slip!* Everybody knows that girl ain't interested in nothing but M-O-N-E-Y. Hussy! Don't want a man of her own, just wants everybody else's.

I ought to call Mrs. Myers right now. Naw, I'm gonna give this lying shit a piece of my mind! I flap my arms for him to stop, but he zooms right on past. *I know he saw me!* That damn golddigger is laughing at me. Floozy! That's why I quit church. Damn deacons! I see why they named roach bait after them.

I see Junior and his sister walking down the street. They some of the best children I seen in years. Their parents are *strict*. Ain't no kids running that household. Chile, kids will be out of control if you don't put your foot on their necks. Uhmm, I been noticing that his sister been outside checking the screens on her windows lately. I wonder if she heard something? *Well we know she ain't crazy enough to climb out of it.* Maybe I ought to tell her Father so he can check them screens too. Something's on her mind if she's checking them that often. I wave and go inside the house.

I hear loud singing coming from the back yard. There he is, regular as clockwork, drinking his days away since his wife left. I saw his wife's ex-husband come over one night then she was gone. Poof!

They say she was into some freaky massaging shit and he put her out. I don't know though. She seemed so *nice.* Goes to show you, things ain't what they seem. I bet she left him and went back to her ex. Well, have a drink on me, brotherman.

I ease my old bones into my favorite easy chair. These folk, these folks. I think the devil must have sent out promotional flyers to get into Hell early again. I sigh and take a sip of my toddy. Shit. My neighborhood, your neighborhood. Ain't no difference. Don't matter if it's hoity-toity or the ghetto. *Ain't no different!* The more things change the more they stay the same. You can move, but you can't escape it. Folks are the same everywhere. Same shit, different place, *somewhere* in America.